DEATH WALKS SKID ROW

Sunset Boulevard, 1975: Two men are speeding home from a party on a night that will haunt them forever. Despite the dangerously wet roads, both passenger and driver are very drunk. Thirty years later on Los Angeles's Skid Row, a homeless man is found dead in an alley. Discovering several disturbing connections, reporter Ramona Rios and a man known on Skid Row only as 'the governor' set out on separate paths to unveil the truth, but are brought together to face a perilous web of power, manipulation and deceit.

MICHAEL MALLORY

DEATH WALKS SKID ROW

Complete and Unabridged

LINFORD
Leicester

First published in Great Britain

First Linford Edition
published 2019

A catalogue record for this book is available
from the British Library.

ISBN 978–1–4448–4233–3

Published by
F. A. Thorpe (Publishing)
Anstey, Leicestershire

Set by Words & Graphics Ltd.
Anstey, Leicestershire
Printed and bound in Great Britain by
T. J. International Ltd., Padstow, Cornwall

This book is printed on acid-free paper

Prologue

Sunset Boulevard,
Los Angeles, California
June 29, 1975
1:13 a.m.

The unseasonal thunderstorm that had drenched Los Angeles, which came as a surprise to just about everyone in the city (even the TV weathercasters), had made the streets dangerously wet and slick.

There was no opposing traffic on Sunset Boulevard as the midnight-blue Jag roared through Rustic Canyon, one of the darkest, curviest, most wooded sections of street in the entirety of L.A. That was a good thing since the car was weaving erratically between the two lanes, straightening the curves wherever possible. The two men in the car, the driver and the passenger, were very drunk, having recently staggered out of a party at a mansion in Pacific Palisades.

1

'Jesus, Bone, slow down,' Mac said.

'Wha' for?' the driver drawled. 'Nobody else out here this time o' night.'

'That's no reason to kill us.'

Bone began clucking like a chicken.

'C'mon, man, the road's wet . . . hey, look out!'

A deer — a big one, with a sizeable rack — was suddenly silhouetted in the road in front of them. The driver made an attempt to brake, but the deer did not wait to see what happened; it leapt away into the trees.

'Christ, that was too close,' Mac sighed. 'Now you gonna slow down?'

'Aw, where's your sense of adventure?'

If anything, the car picked up speed.

Mac tried again. 'Bone, think about it this way: when you drive slower, you save gas. They say it's gonna go up to sixty cents a gallon by the end of the summer. You wanna keep havin' to fill up every other day at sixty cents a gallon?'

The Jag slid off the roadway onto the shoulder, doing nearly seventy. Bone wrenched it back onto the pavement.

'Jesus, we're gonna die!' Mac cried.

'Oh, ye of little balls,' the driver sang.

The two were still arguing three-quarters of a mile down Sunset, when the stopped station wagon appeared on the right shoulder. 'Looks like someone's in trouble,' Mac said.

'Hey, wanna see how close I can get to that car?' Bone asked, grinning.

'No, c'mon, man, don't do it. Just slow down and . . . *Jesus!*'

A second later Mac screamed and threw his hands up over his eyes and only opened them again when he heard the gut-busting laughter coming from the driver.

'What the hell is wrong with you, man?' Mac screamed. 'I thought you were gonna plow right into that car!'

'I wasn't going to hit it,' Bone insisted. 'I must've missed it by, what, a half-inch?'

'Christ.'

Bone laughed again. 'Man, you should have seen yourself! Thought you were going to pee your pants!'

'I'm not sure I didn't. Hey, is that someone walking in the road?'

Bone saw her too. She was a young

woman, maybe early twenties, wearing a peasant blouse and bellbottoms, and holding a section of newspaper over her head as futile protection against the rain. When she turned to see the Jaguar coming toward her, she raised the paper and waived, as though to flag it down. 'Wanna scare her?' he asked.

'Oh, no, man, don't . . . '

Ignoring his friend, Bone pointed the car straight toward her and gunned it.

The woman's eyes widened insanely as she saw that the car was heading straight for her. She tried to run, but slipped on the wet pavement.

Bone tried to swerve away from her at the last minute.

He didn't make it.

The Jaguar's rear wheels skidded out and the car smashed into the woman full force, plowing her under.

The car made a complete donut before sliding to a stop, and was now sideways across Sunset Boulevard.

'What happened?' Bone muttered.

'What do you *think* happened?' Mac screamed, his voice high and shaking.

'You just ran somebody over!'

'I can't have.'

'*Jesus,* Bone!'

'Maybe I missed her.'

'How? *How?* Didn't you feel the thump?'

'Get out and look.'

'Me? Why me?'

''Cause I'm gonna . . . ' Bone got the drivers's door open just in time to keep from vomiting all over his expensive leather upholstery.

'Oh god,' Mac moaned. He got out of the car and walked around it on shaky legs.

The bleeding, woman-shaped heap was only a few yards away.

At first he thought she might be moving, but then realized that it was only his vision that was moving, reeling from the shock and the alcohol. Cautiously, and with an unsure stomach himself, he approached the figure and turned it over.

There was no question she was dead. Nobody could have survived the wounds to her head and face, which were crushed.

But her eyes were still open in the rain,

5

and staring at him meaninglessly.

Mac's body turned to ice and he sank down onto his knees, muttering, 'Oh god, oh god, oh god, oh god . . . '

As soon as his legs would support him again, he got up and went back to the car. The driver was back inside and the engine was running.

'Is she . . . ?' Bone asked.

'Yeah,' Mac said numbly.

'What was she doing out here anyway?'

'That was probably her car stopped on the shoulder back there. It must have broken down. She was probably trying to find a house, or somebody to help her. I don't *know* what she was doing out here! But what are we gonna do?'

'Get the hell out of here, that's what.'

'But we can't — '

Bone was already straightening the car on the street. The Jag was not handling particularly well, having been damaged by the impact, but it drove.

'You're just gonna leave her there like that?' Mac asked.

'There's nothing we can do for her now,' Bone said. 'We have to think of ourselves. I'm sure as hell not sticking around for the damn cops to show up.'

Mac suddenly felt as sober as he had ever been in his life. And while he could not speak for Bone on that score, he noticed that his friend's driving had improved.

Neither spoke for several miles until they had reached the edge of the Sunset Strip, which was filled with traffic as a result of the clubs and bars having just let out.

Finally, Bone said, 'We really lucked out, you know that? Nobody saw anything. No other cars out here. No witnesses.'

'I wouldn't say it was luck,' Mac uttered.

'Here's what's gonna happen. I'll drop you off and then take the car home and lock it up in the garage until I can get it fixed. If anybody says anything about the damage, I'll say I hit a deer. Only I'll say I hit it in Laurel Canyon or someplace. I'll drive the Lincoln for a while.'

'Cops aren't stupid, Bone.'

'Listen to me! That is the story. That's what you will say if anybody asks you. You stick to it and no one will ever find out.

Pretty soon it will be like this never happened. You got it? *You got it?*'

'Jesus, Bone . . . '

'It *never* happened. You hear me? It never happened. Say it.'

'It never happened.'

The driver paused, then said, 'What never happened, man?'

Mac wanted to laugh. On some level, he needed to laugh. He tried to laugh. But he couldn't. He just couldn't.

He wondered if he'd ever laugh again.

1

Except for being stuck in an elevator with Harve 'Hot-Stuff' Huffert, the David Cop-A-Feel sports reporter at her station, the last place Ramona Rios wanted to be right now was standing on a vacant lot in the heart of Skid Row. Even by L.A. standards it was hot, the hottest day of the year so far, ninety-nine degrees or better, which made this part of downtown smell even worse. The ever-present stench of urine from the alleys and gutters mingled with the reek of old stale grease that was coming from the grungy fry joint across the street, making anyone who would be watching her report glad no one had yet invented smell-o-vision.

Ramona squinted in the bright sunlight

as she surveyed the blighted neighborhood. She understood this was part of her job. If she ever hoped to work her way up to the anchor chair, she had to do the field work. Still, she couldn't help but notice that pert, audibly-blonde Kristina Borkland was never sent anywhere but the West Side or the richer parts of the San Fernando Valley to do live reports.

At least she had the satisfaction of knowing she wouldn't have to return home to her cheating boyfriend Lonnie that night; she had thrown him out over the weekend.

'Okay, Ramona, give me a sound check,' said Larry Frank, a veteran of L.A. news who was her entire crew. The two were in the worst section of downtown to cover a non-event: the press conference to announce plans for a new commercial and residential complex that promised to revitalize the area.

Yet again.

Glancing down at her notes, Ramona held up her microphone and said, 'Testing, one, two, three . . . this is Ramona Rios. I'm standing here in hellish

10

heat on the corner of Sixth and San Pedro — the armpit of Los Angeles — waiting to enlighten you about a new scheme by rich people to vacuum up city funding, by which I mean your tax dollars.'

Larry Frank groaned. 'You know, kiddo,' he began, 'one of these days you're going to step in it up to your ankles doing that sort of thing. What if the switcher in the booth had accidentally hit the wrong button and sent you out over the airwaves saying that?'

'He didn't, did he?'

'No, but — '

Ramona flashed her perfect, dimpled smile. 'Then what's the problem?'

'All I'm saying is you need to be a little more careful.' He put the video camera up to his eye. 'We're going live in two minutes.'

'God, I wish I could do something about that sun,' Ramona complained, holding her notes over her eyes. 'I don't want to squint all the way through this. How about if I cheat into this shadow?' She stepped into a dark patch cast by a competing station's news truck that was parked on the street.

'Then you become a silhouette. Get back on mark and stop complaining. I'm not responsible for staging this event looking into the sun.'

Ramona knew who was: Nick Cantone, the billionaire developer and city power-broker who was the force behind 'Phoenix Terrace,' the proposed reconstruction of this entire city block. Maybe not Cantone personally, but someone from his office. Probably the same staffer who had ordered that all the homeless be bused out of the area so none would be seen on camera for the grand press event ceremony.

At least according to the rumor Ramona had heard.

'A minute-thirty,' Larry said.

Ramona was beginning to perspire, which was bad television. 'Executive decision, Larry,' she said, stepping into a narrow shady patch cast by a tall tree. 'If I'm in shadow, fix it.'

'Dammit, Ramona! The point of the shot is to have the dignitaries' platform in

12

the background behind you!'

'Not if I can't open my eyes! C'mon, they made me the segment producer, so I'm producing. Film the platform on b-roll.'

'Jesus,' Larry muttered to himself. In the thirty-one years that he had been working at KPAC, starting back in the days when all remotes were shot on 16mm film and cut by hand, he had seen dozens of reporters come and go, some good, some mediocre, some dedicated journalists, and some telegenic airheads like that Borkland bimbo. Ramona Rios definitely had the chops to be a reporter, and she was damned easy to look at, but it didn't take a psychic to predict that her jones for taking chances was someday going to turn around and bite her in that cute little butt.

'Fine, your call,' he sighed, adjusting the camera's position. 'Thirty seconds, by the way.'

Through her earpiece Ramona heard the voice of Matt Stevens, the News at Eleven anchor.

Larry flashed his free hand three times,

indicating fifteen seconds, though at this point Ramona would be taking her cue from Matt's throw to her.

' ... announcement of a major development in downtown Los Angles,' she heard him say. 'Ramona Rios is on the scene. Ramona, what's happening?'

'Matt,' Ramona began, 'up until now, this section of downtown Los Angeles, which for the last sixty years has been known as Skid Row, has defied redevelopment efforts. But State Assemblyman Adam Henry and developer Nick Cantone are planning to put an end to that curse. Very shortly, Assemblyman Henry and Mr. Cantone, along with representatives of the city's Community Redevelopment Agency, will be here to break ground for Phoenix Terrace, a new hundred-million dollar residential and shopping complex that they hope will be the pivot point for this long-depressed area. While some city leaders, including several on the city council and, it has been rumored, Mayor Alberto Soto himself, remain skeptical that enough people can be induced to make this area their home, Mr. Cantone has long maintained — '

14

Just then the voice of Jess Kalman, the director, could be heard through her earpiece shouting, 'Aw, crap, look in the background!'

Instinctively, Ramona turned around to see what was happening. Two street men were shuffling up behind her. One was young, black, and still had definable clothing, which implied that he had not long been homeless. The other was older, probably Caucasian, though it was hard to tell through the sun-baked dirt and scraggly gray beard on his face. His tattered clothes were all a uniform leaden-brown color, dyed from the experience of living on the streets for a long time. They did not speak to each other but merely walked side by side like exhausted soldiers after a battle.

'Don't turn away from the camera!' Kalman was screaming. 'Jesus! Larry, go somewhere else!'

'Stay on me, Larry,' Ramona said. Then starting to walk toward the men, she continued. 'It is well known that there are some ten-thousand homeless people living in Skid Row, and yet these two that you see behind me are the only residents of this area that I have seen today. It makes one wonder if the rumors I've heard, that the homeless had been swept from the area in anticipation of this event today, can really be true.'

'Ramona, what the hell are you doing?' Kalman shouted.

She ignored him.

'Ramona Rios, KPAC News at Eleven, can I speak with you gentlemen?' she asked.

Forced to follow her lead, Larry now made the two homeless men the center-piece of the shot. Neither, though, seemed aware that they were being photographed. The older and dirtier of the two suddenly tilted his head up and appeared to look sideways into the camera lens, but Larry was quickly able to discern that the man was not really seeing him. The guy had a dead left eye which turned out too far to the side to be functional.

'Have you been asked to leave the area?' Ramona asked them. Neither replied. 'Have your friends been evacuated out?'

'Friends?' the one with the crooked eye shouted. Then he began to laugh.

Turning back to the camera, her head shaking sadly, Ramona said, 'Matt, this area is the home to these two gentlemen and countless others like them. The question that remains unanswered is not so much whether more affluent people are going to respond to the gentrification of Skid Row, but what is going to happen to this area's current residents, like these two, once the Phoenix Terrace is opened for business? Where are they going to go? Live from Skid Row, this is Ramona Rios. Matt, back to you in the studio.'

'Aw, Christ, camera one,' Kalman's voice commanded through the earpieces.

Once she had received the weak 'clear' from Jess, Ramona took down her microphone and walked to the cameraman. 'Do you think 'depressed' was the right word to describe this place?' she asked. 'Should I have said 'blighted?''

'Hey, don't ask me, you're the segment producer,' Larry Frank replied, with a shrug.

What he was thinking was: *Been nice*

working with you, kiddo.

Two police officers now appeared to shoo away the homeless men as Assemblyman Adam Henry looked on in concern. At the platform, three men in suits and a smartly dressed woman began to ascend the small step unit to take their seats on the dais.

A limo pulled up on the street and Ramona saw Nick Cantone step out. His gleaming hair, the color of a newly-minted quarter, made him one of the easiest 'spots' in the city. He was followed by Assemblyman Adam Henry, who was tanned, trim, and looked every inch the action hero he had played on television and in film before turning to politics. As they made their way to the platform, which was now surrounded by a half-dozen LAPD officers, a young, rabbitish technician did a sound check on a microphone at the podium in the middle of the dais. Other news crews, both television and radio, started to gather around.

'Okay, Larry,' Ramona said, dabbing at her sweating face with a Kleenex, 'let's get this over with.'

Yep, you're going places, kiddo, Larry Frank thought as he followed her over to the ceremony platform. *Starting this afternoon.*

2

The middle-aged, gray-haired, bushy-bearded African American street man strode onto his familiar corner. The sun was high in the sky and it was a hot day, but the weather mattered little in terms of the man's wardrobe. He would have worn the same old, frayed, green slacks, once-white shirt, and scuffed, faded leather jacket no matter whether it was triple-digit Fahrenheit, pouring rain, or snowing. Of course, it never did the latter in Los Angeles. Strangely, though, even though the man wore the same clothing day after day, month after month, year after year, his clothes never gave off the same reek of sweat and filth as did the clothing of so many other denizens of the streets. Those on Skid Row who knew him — and there were many — could not explain this phenomenon, if they were even cognizant enough to care. It was just one of the mysteries that surrounded the man known only as 'the governor.'

He had just made it out of the alley beside the Star Liquor Mart on Seventh when the young man who called himself Aspen came running up to him. 'Hey, Governor, you don't happen to have a quarter on you, do you?' Aspen asked.

Nobody knew if Aspen was actually his name or the place from whence he had come. He was tall, strapping, blond, and blue-eyed, and had only shown up on Skid Row sometime in the last week.

'A quarter, you say?' the governor replied.

'Yeah, so I can get a few smokes. Mario in the store there sells them three for a buck, and I've got the seventy-five already, so I need another quarter.'

'And you're coming to me?'

'C'mon, man, you always seem to have a little spare change.'

Reaching into his pants pocket, the governor withdrew a quarter, which glinted like platinum in the sun. Before handing it to the kid, he turned it over and saw that it was one of those special commemorative state quarters — Texas, to be precise. 'Haven't seen this one,' he muttered.

'What's special about it?'

'Oh, it's one of those fifty state quarters. Texas. I haven't seen Texas.'

'Why do they even do that?'

'I don't know. Makes them collectable, I guess.'

'Collectable,' Aspen sneered, taking the coin from him. 'Some folks got so much money they can collect it. It ain't fair.'

'Life ain't fair, son,' the governor replied.

'Yeah, well, thanks, man.' The young man slipped the coin into the pocket of his dirty jeans and headed for the liquor store.

Something about Aspen fascinated the governor. Wherever he had come from, whatever situation it was that had deposited him on the streets, it must have been hard and dispiriting, because the man actually seemed happy to be where he was. That was not unknown, of course. Many of the guys, and even some of the women, lived on the streets by choice. They were escaping a harsh or crippling environment, or thought they were, or else had not realized that the environment was within their own mind, and the extreme realities of street life only made it seem like they were escaping. Others, of course, were not in their own minds. They should be institutionalized or hospitalized, or at least under constant medical supervision; instead they were turned out to fend for themselves in the name of 'shrinking government.' But none of that seemed to apply to Aspen. His was a different story, and someday the governor would get it, the way he got everybody's story, eventually.

Aspen was now coming out of the Star Liquor Mart puffing happily away on one of his illicit smokes. The governor was about to let Aspen go about his business when he saw the young man stop suddenly. Even from a distance of a city block, the governor could tell that he was tensing. There was probably a police presence down there and the kid wasn't used to it yet. He was looking at something, something the governor couldn't see. Something that was in the alley between a flophouse apartment building and a vacant building that used to be a cleaner's (back when people in the area had the money and ambition to stay clean). Slowly, Aspen started stalking whatever it was — cautiously, the way a cat will stalk something that it cannot quite see, ever-ready to spring back should it prove to be dangerous or threatening. The governor's complete attention was now on the younger streetman. He started sauntering his way, just in case Aspen required help. At sixty-one, the governor was not the greatest help in a fight but he was not useless either.

As the governor watched, Aspen crept far enough into the alleyway to disappear from sight. Then the governor heard a cry, and started jogging toward the young man. He got to the entrance of the alley just in time to see Aspen dash out. When he saw the governor, he said, 'Dead!'

'Who?'

'I don't know.' Aspen directed the older man to a pile of rags leaned up against the side of the apartment building — a pile of rags with the remnants of a man inside. The governor approached the figure and pushed it with the toe of his battered shoe. A litter of rats fanned out from it, scurrying over the trash in the alley. The figure reeked of human waste and urine, which might ordinarily be an indication that one was looking at a dead body, but not on the streets where many people reeked of human waste and urine. Kneeling down, the governor took the figure's hand and felt for a pulse.

Pulse be damned; nobody could be that cold and still be alive.

'Do you know who it is?' Aspen asked.

Carefully turning the body toward him, the governor studied the face. One of the dead man's eyes was closed and the other open. 'Yeah, I know him. It's Jimmy.'

'Jimmy who?'

The governor looked up at the younger man. 'What difference does it make? That's like asking Aspen who?'

'All right, all right. Hey, that isn't the little guy with the gammy eye, is it?'

'Yep. Jim was blind in one eye. I was always afraid he was going to walk in front of a car because of it.'

'Maybe that's what happened.'

'I don't think so.'

The governor carefully moved the front of Jimmy's dirt-encrusted army surplus jacket to reveal a shirt that had once been khaki, but was now brown with filth. The bottom half of the shirt, covering the dead man's belly, was stained red and still damp.

'Jesus!' Aspen whispered, blanching. 'Why would . . . ?'

The governor stood up. 'You're new here. Some people out here would try to kill you over a pair of shoes. Some just because their deck's missing a few aces. People get dropped off in the middle of the night by their hospitals when their insurance runs out. Suddenly they got no meds, and less control. The whys don't even matter much, son. This is Skid Row, and it's never a beautiful day in this neighborhood. You want to stay here, you're going to have to get used to that.'

'Why do you stay here, then?' Aspen asked.

The governor knew damn well why he was here, but he was not about to explain it to the kid. Certainly not now. 'Why do you think?' he said, his mouth crinkling into a smile. 'My mansion in Beverly Hills is being painted and I can't stand the smell. Now you stay here with the body. I'll go find a cop.'

'How do you even get a cop down here?' Aspen asked as the governor started walking away.

'You tell one of these shop owners to call them,' the governor answered. 'Having a dead body lying around the place tends to be bad for business, even on Skid Row.' He walked to the Star Liquor Mart, where Aspen had bought his smokes, and asked the clerk to call the police. But the young-ish, Pakistani man behind the counter refused, claiming it was none of his business.

'Look, the cops aren't going to care if you sell sticks individually under the counter,' the governor said.

'I don't know what you are talking about.'

'Right, you don't know. Give me the damn phone then, and I'll call them.'

'I have only a cell phone. How do I know you won't steal it?'

'Friend, if I wanted to steal something,

I'd steal something with street value. Like this.' The governor picked a twelve-pack of Bud off of a stacked display and started to leave.

'Stop!' the clerk called. 'Stop, you thief!' He leapt over the counter and pulled out his cell phone, and jabbed a button for a pre-set number. 'Police!' he cried loudly. 'My store is being robbed!'

As the clerk was giving the address, the governor smiled, turned back, and set back the twelve-pack. 'It's not robbery unless I leave the premises,' he said, after the clerk had hung up. 'Until then I'm just shopping. But thanks for calling the cops like I asked.'

'Get out! Go away! Do not come back!'

'Pleasure doing business with you.'

The governor strolled back out into the hot day, which somehow seemed to have gotten hotter while he was inside the store, and looked down the street. There was now a collection of people standing around Aspen; some staring into the alley, some staring off into space, and one leaning heavily on a walker. News traveled fast in Skid Row. Within minutes the police car arrived in front of the store, and the governor watched as the officer in the shotgun seat got out of the black-and-white. It was Officer Hugo Velasquez, which was both good and bad news. He was about thirty, a shade too old to be a rookie, but still too young to be a veteran. While not a bully, Velasquez was not one to be pushed. He'd never been break-your-arm mean, but was not particularly friendly either. There were frown lines on his handsome brown face, which he might have been born with for all the governor knew, and a small scar above his left eyebrow — a brand from growing up on gang turf.

Down the street, some of the row's denizens began to shuffle away, as though they did not want to be spotted committing the crime of existing.

Velasquez walked up to the governor, who was standing just outside the market, and glared at him. 'Dammit, Gov, don't tell me you're the one ripping this place off,' he said.

'Absolutely not,' the governor said. 'You can search me if you like.'

'And get fleas? Hell no.'

By now the driver of the car, an older officer with graying sandy hair, stepped past them and into the market, only to re-emerge a half-minute later. 'The clerk phoned in a false alarm,' he told Velasquez. 'Waste of time.'

'Not quite,' the governor said, directing their attention down the street. 'There's a body down there.'

'A body?' said the older officer, whose nametag ID'd him as Walpole. 'Did you find him or did you kill him?'

'Neither. That young fellow down there, the blond one, found him.'

'Streeter?' Velasquez asked.

The governor nodded. 'New kid on the block. The victim's been down here for years. Went by the name of Jimmy. I think you're going to need to bring in homicide on this one.'

'We are, are we?' Officer Walpole asked. 'You going to stick around to make a statement?'

'Of course,' the governor answered. 'I'll tell you what I know, but it ain't much. The young fellow standing down there is the one who found him.'

Walpole got back into the cruiser, turned on the siren and flashers, and drove down the block to where Aspen was standing. He pulled to the curb again, leaving the lights on, while Velasquez and the governor followed on foot.

'You'll tell us everything you know about this, right?' Velasquez asked.

'If I knew anything, I'd tell you. You know that. Where'd you get your new partner?'

'He got himself sent to us from the Valley. I'm not sure what he did to piss off the Valley so badly. What's your take on the newbie that found the vic?'

'He calls himself Aspen, and he hasn't been on any street very long. Pretty green.'

'You make him as the killer?'

'Not unless he was an Oscar-winning actor before hitting the row. He looked like he was going to pass out when he saw blood, and I don't think he was faking it.'

Velasquez smiled, though the frown lines did not soften. 'Maybe,' he said. 'But who knows? There might be more than one Oscar-winner wandering around out here.'

As they reached the alley now, Officer Walpole was calling for back-up and requesting the medical examiner. 'Homicide's on the way,' Walpole told Velasquez, without looking at him. Neither was he looking at Aspen, though the young man, now over his shock, appeared to hang intently on every word the policeman spoke like he was mentally recording it.

'What's the cause of death?' Velasquez asked.

'Appears to be a knife,' Walpole said. 'Good, professional job too, quick and clean.'

'Why would a professional want to kill a bum?'

'Not our problem. Homicide's on the way.'

A few minutes later an unmarked car pulled up, and a tall, wiry plainclothesman with thinning, sandy hair leapt out and was directed to the body.

'Don't go anywhere,' Office Walpole told Aspen. 'The detective's going to want to talk with you.'

After conferring with the two uniformed officers, the sandy-haired man approached Aspen who was standing next to the governor. 'Detective Darrell Knight,' he said, flashing his badge. 'I understand that it was you who found the body.'

'Yeah, I found it,' Aspen replied.

Knight led him through a series of questions about the discovery, and what he did, and lobbed a few at the governor as well, mostly routine. Then he said, 'Okay, gentlemen, let's see your hands.'

'Huh?' Aspen asked.

'Hands, hands, those things at the end of your arms, with the fingers and all, stick them out.'

With a muted smile, the governor did so, palms up. After a second, Aspen followed suit.

'Turn 'em over,' the detective instructed, and both men did.

'Yeah, okay. You guys can beat it. Tell your friends to stay away from here, too, until we get things sorted out.' With that, Detective Knight turned away and went back to the alley.

'Come with me,' the governor said,

taking Aspen by the arm and leading him back toward the market.

'What was that all about?' the young man asked.

'He was looking for blood. He wanted to see if either of us could have been the killer.'

'That's stupid. If I had killed somebody and gotten blood on myself, I'd have washed it off before the cops came.'

'You would?'

'Well, sure. Wouldn't you?'

The governor stopped walking and held his hands up in front of Aspen. 'What do you see on my hands?' he asked.

'Dirt, mostly,' the younger man answered. 'And calluses.' Then a look of realization played across his face. 'Oh, I get it. It's not possible to wash off blood and leave the dirt, right? So the cop was looking to see if our hands were dirty or recently washed. Is that it?'

The governor gave the younger man a long, quizzical stare.

'What's the matter?' Aspen asked. 'Why are you looking at me like that?'

'Just trying to decide about you,' the

34

governor replied.

'Decide what? Hey, man, you don't think I had anything to do with that guy's death, do you?'

'I try not to think, son. 'Sides, it's too damn hot to think.'

With that, the governor walked away into the heat of the afternoon, completely unaware that he was, at that moment, being photographed.

3

Two days had passed since finding the body on Skid Row, and while he hadn't forgotten about the dead homeless guy, Detective Darrell Knight had too many other open cases to lavish a lot of time on that one.

Having finished his fifth cup of coffee of the morning, Knight had just gotten up from his desk at Central division to go to the bathroom, when his phone rang. Sighing, he picked it up and said, 'Knight, make it quick' into the mouthpiece.

'Darrell, Ben Yamahiro.' Yamahiro worked in the L.A. County Coroner's office. 'Got a minute?'

'Can you make it thirty seconds? I'm about to flood the floor.'

There was a chuckle at the other end of the line.

'I'll be quick. Can you come down to the morgue?'

'To see what?'

'That John Doe who came in a few days ago, the street bum?'

'What about him?' Knight asked, trying to ignore the serious complaint his bladder was making.

'I'd rather tell you in person if you don't mind.'

'Okay, Ben. I'll be down later this afternoon.' Knight hung up the phone and rushed away from his desk.

Since making Detective II four months prior, Knight's caseload had increased exponentially. He sometimes wondered if all the murderers in the city had not been waiting just for him to get his bump. Leslie, his wife, wondered even more. What he wondered on a daily basis was how much longer Leslie was going to put up with his no longer being around most evenings and weekends.

Because of the casework that had to be dealt with before he could safely leave the office, it was nearly two hours later before he made it down to the coroner's building in Boyle Heights. Ben Yamahiro, a small man of about forty, who wore TV-sized glasses, was waiting for him. 'I didn't hear about a requisition for canoes at Parker Center,' he joked.

'No thanks to you,' Knight said. 'So what's up with our John Doe?'

'There are some things I want to show you.'

'On the body?'

'No, back at my office.'

Once they had arrived at the cluttered office, Yamahiro laid out a series of digital pictures on his desk for Knight to study. 'Well, this is him, all right,' the detective said. 'I recognize the wound.'

'How about this one?' Yamahiro asked, laying down another set of pictures. Upon perusing them, Knight frowned.

'Or these two.'

'These are all different guys,' Knight said.

'Mm-hmm. Five in all, and all homeless. You can see now why I contacted you.'

Even the greenest rookie would have been able to see that the wounds on every one of the corpses in the photos were identical, varying only slightly in their positions on the bodies. But the angle of the cut, the apparent depth, and the size of the opening argued for the exact same weapon, and very likely the same hand wielding the weapon. 'Where were the bodies of these others found?'

'All over the city. One even in Santa Monica,' Yamahiro answered.

'And over how long a period of time?'

'Two weeks.'

'Two weeks?'

Yamahiro pointed to one photo in particular. 'This is the first we received. Your fellow is the most recent.'

'Why didn't you contact us before there were five?'

'I did. Up until now, no one else seemed to care.'

Knight sat down in the room's guest chair and exhaled audibly. 'So, according to this, we've got some nut running all through the city, maybe even the county, stabbing homeless men.'

'Seems that way,' the medical examiner said.

'There's no way this is coincidence, is there?'

Yamahiro shook his head. 'In the notes

I made upon each examination, I noticed that each time there was evidence of the attacker twisting the knife once it had been inserted into the abdomen. The damage to the tissue is identical in every case.'

'A serial killer who specializes in bums. Christ.'

'What better way to remain invisible than to kill invisible victims?'

'And who knows how long he's been at it?' Knight added. 'I mean, we have evidence of five, but how many others might there have been that weren't connected, or even discovered?'

Yamahiro shrugged, then looked up at Knight with a patient smile. 'The larger question would seem to be . . . how many more will there be in the future?'

'I trust you will keep me informed of any new ones that come in. Even if they're not in my jurisdiction.'

'Of course.'

'Great.' Knight rose from the chair and took a final glance at the photos. 'I'll need any paperwork you have on these guys, too.'

'Shouldn't be a problem.'

'Okay, Ben.' Knight held out his hand which the other man shook. 'I hope you'll forgive me if I don't exactly thank you for dropping this on me.'

'I thought it was something that should not be ignored.'

'Yeah. It's just too bad that none of these poor bastards will ever realize that someone is finally not ignoring them. I'll find my way out.'

Knight headed back toward the entrance of the building, passing the gift shop on the way. *Only in L.A.*, he thought, *does the county morgue have a souvenir store.* He was going to have to report what Yamahiro had shown him to his lieutenant, but he could not predict the outcome.

How do you convince a bureaucracy to find a way to protect people that nobody wanted protected in the first place?

★ ★ ★

Ramona Rios looked at the man across the desk with murder in her eyes. 'You can't do this,' she said with dangerous quiet.

41

'I'm sorry, Ramona,' Jason Hulme said, 'but we have to maximize our resources here at the station. In talking it over with Bob, we have decided that you will be best utilized on Sunday mornings.'

'When no one watches,' she said, looking back and forth between Hulme, the station manager, and Robert Bauman, the news director. Bauman looked slightly uncomfortable, though Hulme, behind the veneer of professionalism, appeared to be enjoying himself. Even though the air conditioning in Hulme's enormous office was on full blast, she felt warm. She turned her gaze at the paunchy, prematurely white-haired man who had been KPAC's news honcho for nearly a quarter-century. 'Bob, I'm the best field reporter you have, and you know it.'

Bauman kept his eyes down. 'That's why we want you on weekends,' he said. 'We want to beef up the weekend coverage.'

'That's bull and you know it,' she charged.

'Frankly, Ramona, I don't understand your reluctance,' Hulme said smoothly.

He was a carrot-haired Brit who had been at the station a little over a year, having been installed by ComCorp, the media conglomerate that had taken over the station last year. Hulme's task was to transform the indie broadcaster into a serious competitor for L.A.'s CBS, ABC, NBC and Fox affiliates. 'This is a chance to work your way into the anchor chair.'

'The *weekend* anchor chair.'

'It's still an anchor position,' Bauman said.

'It's a second-string anchor position.'

Hulme leaned back in his leather executive chair. 'My dear Ms. Rios, you have been with this station exactly five months, during which time your work has been of a consistently high quality. We are very pleased with what you've been doing, but let's not get carried away. You really think you can waltz into a weeknight anchor job after only five months in the field?'

'Jaac DuPree did field work for three years before becoming anchor,' Bauman said.

'Exactly,' Hulme went on. 'Here we are

trying to put you on the fast track, and all you can do is complain about it.'

'Okay, fine,' she said. 'You want to give me the weekend anchor chair, fine. There's no reason I can't do that and my regular weekday field work both.'

'Ramona, please -' Bauman began, but Hulme silenced him with a gesture. Leaning forward in his chair, the station manager glared at the reporter in silence until she blinked and looked away. 'Look at me, Ms. Rios,' he demanded, forcing her gaze back. 'You seem to be under the impression that this is negotiable. It is not. You are being moved to weekends. That is our decision.'

She attempted to glare back, but Hulme's stare was too cold to hold. 'Robert,' she said, turning to the news director, 'is this really your decision, too?'

'Well, you know, Ramona — '

Hulme cut him off again. 'We are in agreement.'

'This is not fair,' she said, her voice now taking on a beaten tone. 'I'm the one who broke the story about the homeless being bused out of Skid Row for that dedication ceremony, the same story that the *Times* picked up and ran with for the next week. I deserve better than week-ends.'

'*Enough*!' Hulme shouted, startling both Ramona and Bauman. 'Bob, if you can't control your people any better than this, maybe it's time *your* duties change as well!'

'Look, Jason — '

Hulme stood up and leaned over his desk with one hand, while jabbing an index finger at his office door. 'Ramona, half the people out there would get on their knees before me for this kind of opportunity! Meeting's over, get out of here!'

Ramona stared back at him. 'So that's what this is really about.'

'What's really what this is about?'

'Sexual harassment. You heard him, Robert. He wants me on my knees in front of him.'

'Not a word, Bauman,' Hulme commanded. 'That is an outright misrepresentation of my words, not to mention slanderous. If you have any intention of working here at all, in any capacity, Ms. Rios, you will apologize this instant.'

'*Apologize?*' she cried, leaping out of her chair. 'Okay, how's this: I'm sorry I ever came to this amateur station! You'll be hearing from my lawyer!'

Hulme laughed. 'My dear, I spent the better part of yesterday with our legal team, and do you know what they told me? They said your contract isn't worth rolling up and using for a tampon. So don't presume to threaten me.'

Shaking with anger, Ramona turned and stormed toward the office door.

'You leave this way and you leave ComCorp for good,' Hulme said.

'Fine. I don't need ConCrap!' she shouted.

Wrenching the door open, she strode through and swung it shut behind her so violently that one of Hulme's framed pictures fell from the wall.

'Mother of God, Jason,' Bauman said, looking shocked, 'what was that about?'

Hulme was smiling a cobra's smile. 'It was about dealing with a problem. No more Rios, no more problem.'

'You knew she wouldn't accept the weekend gig.'

46

'Of course I did. I know her type. Just like I know your type.'

'My type?'

'Look, Robbo, had I fired her outright, she could have cried wrongful termination, and she might have gotten someone to listen. This way, she walked out on her own. I might even be able to sue her.'

'But she's a damned good reporter — '

'There are hundreds of damned good reporters who would kill to work in a major market. We don't need any prima donnas.'

'Do we need lawsuits?'

'What lawsuits are those?'

Bauman blinked at his boss as though he had suddenly turned into an alien. 'Was I the only one who heard the threat of a sexual harassment lawsuit?'

Still smiling, Hulme came around the desk and put his arm around the shorter, older man. 'Robbo, she can try to sue us for anything she wants. Wrongful termination, sexual harassment, discrimination, whatever. You think any attorney she could produce would stand a chance against ComCorp's legal team? Gloria

Allred would roll on her back and say and 'thank you' by the time our boys were done. We made Rios a good-faith offer of potential career advancement, and she blew up and made some wild accusations, simple as that. It's not like she hasn't got a track record of stepping on toes around here, all of which is documented in her personnel file.'

'Maybe she's a little too ambitious for her own good, but did you have to give her the get-on-your-knees line? Followed by a tampon crack?'

'C'mon, Robbo, that's how you pray. At least that's how I pray. Your people, I don't know.'

Bauman gaped at him. 'Did you just say 'my people'? What's that supposed to mean, my people? You mean Jews? Is that it?'

Hulme's hand squeezed tighter on Bauman's shoulder. 'What I'm trying to impress upon you is that conversations are funny things. I say 'your people,' and you hear anti-Semitism. But here's the salient point. Even if I were to call you a washed-up Jew bastard, there's no one here to verify it. With only two people in a conversation, it's one person's word against another's.'

'Maybe, maybe not,' Bauman said. 'But you're forgetting that I was here when you were talking to Ramona. I was the witness. I can offer verification.'

'But you won't.'

'I'm not going to lie for you.'

'Who said anything about lying for me? Did I say anything about lying?' He let go of Bauman and returned to his desk. 'By the way, Robert, how old are you?'

'How old?'

'Yeah, you know, your age? The amount of time you've been breathing on your own?'

'I'm sixty-four, why?'

'Hmmmm,' Hulme muttered. 'Early retirement age.'

'I have no intention of retiring.'

'Of course not. Thing is, I had a memo from corporate a week ago about mandatory retirement age for employees. Naturally, I'd hate to lose you, but you know corporate. They make a decision, it's out of my hands. I could, of course, fight to keep you, tell them you're irreplaceable, all that sort of shite. But I'd have to have something in return.'

Robert Bauman desperately wanted a scotch and water as he calculated the price of his soul. 'What do you want?' he asked.

'Your loyalty, Robbo. The assurance you're a team player.'

'I . . . you know I'm part of the team, Jason,' Bauman said, softly.

'Of course I do,' Hulme replied, grinning. 'And I'll communicate that to corporate. Oh, Christ, I almost forgot, hold on a minute.' Hulme grabbed the phone and buzzed his secretary. 'Keisha, get Dexter on the line, would you?'

Aaron Dexter was head of security for the station.

When Keisha buzzed back, he jabbed another button and said: 'Dex, Jason. I need someone to walk Ramona Rios out of the building. Right, this is her last day. Get all her keys, her card key, everything, and I want her parking spot painted over by tomorrow morning. Get on it right away.' He hung up and turned back to

Bauman. 'I think we're done here, Robbo.'

Bauman was looking at his watch. 'It's 3:45, Jason. We're on the air at 5:00, and I was planning on running Ramona's piece on the food bank.'

'Is it good?'

'Yes, it's good.'

'Then by all means run it. Let's have her go out on a high note. Tell you what, why don't you write a little note for DuPree about how we're all going to miss our little Ramona and we wish her the best of luck for her future career, yibbity-yibbity-yibbity. Now go on, get back to work.'

Bauman was only too glad to be get out of Hulme's office. *Just get me through to seven o'clock*, he thought, *and then get me a nice double Dewars*. But at the door he turned back. 'You know something, Jason?' he said. 'I started in this business right when Nixon became president. My early career was shaped by stories like Vietnam and Watergate.'

'Lovely,' Hulme said, 'but is there a point?'

51

'Yeah. The point is, a lot of people get into journalism, get their feet wet, maybe get their arm hairs singed a little bit, and then get the hell out. I stayed in it, chiefly so I could go after people like you.'

Hulme smiled. 'Well, isn't it amazing how age changes one?'

'Yeah,' Bauman said, turning back toward the door. 'Isn't it?'

By this time, Ramona Rios was all the way down the hall. She stopped to get a drink from the drinking fountain, and then kicked the wall beside it, accomplishing nothing except hurting her toe, and causing a few people in the hallway to stop talking and look her way. Most, realizing it was Ramona, just smiled and went back about their business.

She knew the game they were playing, and she knew why, though it depressed her that Robert had gone along with it — unless, of course, he didn't know what was going to happen. Even so, he knew her well enough to understand that she would never take a demotion, which was what putting her on Sunday mornings amounted to. God, that's where you *started* people! This had to be Hulme's doing, and it had to be a result of her ad-libbing on the Skid Row development story, which had prompted some vehement pushback from both Nick Cantone's office and Assemblyman Henry.

But she was reporting the news, dammit. The *Times* piece had confirmed it. And she had been there first.

Looking up, Ramona saw Aaron Dexter, for whom she had developed an early dislike, and two uniformed security guards, coming her way. She doubted they were simply going to the water fountain. Dexter, a very large African-American with a shaved head and a neatly trimmed moustache, stepped up to her and smiled. 'Don't make this any harder on yourself than it has to be, sugar,' he said.

'Funny thing, Aaron,' she said, smiling back, 'I was about to say the same thing to you. I'm sure you wouldn't want to be personally named in the lawsuit I'm planning to file against this station.'

The smile on Dexter's face fell away. 'I'm just following orders.'

'Oh, I know that, but you're also

enjoying it, aren't you? You're going to really enjoy throwing me off the lot.'

'Let's get going.'

'I have to get my stuff from my cubicle.'

With the two guards puppy-dogging behind them, Dexter led Ramona down the hall. She knew that she was probably not going to file an actual suit. The truth was she did not have the kind of money to hire a high-powered attorney. A good chunk of her salary from the station went to support her mother and younger brothers. But maybe the threat alone would raise enough sweat from both Aaron and Hulme to make the bluff worthwhile.

On the way to her cubicle in the newsroom, they passed Larry Frank. 'You were right, Larry,' Ramona called out, 'I should have kept my mouth shut. They're throwing me out.'

'I'm sorry, Ramona,' he called back.

After collecting all of her personal belongings from her cubicle and putting them in a box (which, Ramona noticed, had conveniently appeared on her desk), she let Dexter walk her down to personnel, where she was instructed to sign a series of forms (which had also miraculously been prepared in advance — Hulme's micromanaging technique was nothing if not thorough). For the first time, Ramona wondered what would have happened had she simply accepted the weekend demotion and gone back to her work. Would that have derailed the plans to get rid of her, or would it simply have delayed the inevitable?

But she had not accepted it. She had done precisely what Hulme was expecting her to do, was counting on her doing.

Outside in the parking lot, she relinquished her parking card and was walked to her car, a four-year-old Mustang convertible that she had bought used and paid cash for. It was still a hot day. She dumped the box in the passenger seat and climbed in.

'Ramona,' Aaron Dexter said, 'you can either believe this or call B.S. on it, but I'm not enjoying this at all.'

Putting on a pair of sunglasses, Ramona looked up at him. 'You know something, Aaron? You were never my favorite person, but neither do I think you're a bad guy.' She put her key in the ignition and started the Mustang up. 'So I'm going to give you a piece of advice. Don't fool yourself into thinking that Jason Hulme has any loyalty to anything or anybody but the shareholders. So you watch your back, big man. You might want to invest in a Kevlar vest.'

Throwing it into reverse, Ramona Rios peeled out of the parking spot, and sped toward the gate.

From his glass-walled corner office, Jason Hulme looked down into the parking lot and watched as Ramona's Mustang blazed through the gate for the last time and then disappeared down the street. He smiled. A moment later, his intercom buzzed and Keisha's voice said: 'I have Mr. Cantone on line one.'

Going back to his desk, Hulme jabbed the line, picked up the receiver and said, 'Hey, Nick, how are you? Yeah, that's why I'm calling. Problem solved, she's gone. Yep, almost as though it was scripted. No, don't worry, she's history. She'll be lucky to get a gig doing the weather on

Telemundo, I'm seeing to that. Yeah. Tennis this weekend? Good. See you then.'

As Jason Hulme replaced the phone, he thought: *I wish all problems were this easy.*

4

The horns of three cars blared as the elderly street man dragged himself slowly and painfully across the street, against the light, pushing the metal walker inches ahead of him with every step. The man ignored the cars as if they weren't there. Morning rush hour meant nothing to him. By the time he made it to the opposite curb, the light had changed back to red. One of the drivers, in a Lexus, angrily shouted an epithet through the window as he rolled through the red light.

From the sidewalk, the governor watched the altercation with little interest. What interested him more was the fact that a police car was pulled up to the curb across the street in front of a sundry shop. The officer behind the wheel made no effort to follow the pickup, even though it had run the light and its driver had harassed a pedestrian. Street people were not really considered pedestrians, the governor knew. Instead they were obstacles. But what was the cruiser doing here?

The governor felt a presence beside him and glanced over to see Aspen standing there. In the days since poor Jim's murder he had not seen much of the younger man. Maybe he'd upset the kid by not exonerating him of murder. But the governor didn't seriously suspect Aspen of the killing.

He had other suspicions regarding him.

'Hey, what's up?' the governor asked glancing down at Aspen's hands. Today they were filthy, almost too filthy, as though they had been deliberately soiled.

'Where do people get all those walkers from?' Aspen asked, casually, watching the old man drag himself down the sidewalk.

The governor shrugged. 'Missions. Churches. Who knows? Maybe there's some foundation that provides them to shelters. I probably won't know for certain until I need one.'

'I hope I never do.'

'Hope is a beautiful thing,' the

governor said softly. 'Where you been keepin' yourself?'

'Hmmm? Oh, I found a place to stay over on Gladys. Not too bad.'

'Residential hotel?'

'Yeah.'

The governor smiled. 'When did you move in?'

Aspen held his hand up over his eyes in an attempt to shade them from the sun. 'I don't know, maybe a week and a half ago, first of the month. Why?'

'Let's get in the shade,' the governor said, walking the younger man next to the side of a building which offered them some protection from the direct sunlight. 'My guess is you're paid up for the month, right?'

'Yeah, I, uh, came into enough money to cover it. Why?'

'Because you're going to be out on the twenty-eighth.'

Aspen looked at the man who was the closest thing to a friend he had on the streets. 'What are you talking about?'

'It's called the '28-Day Shuffle,' son. Once you live somewhere more than thirty days you establish legal residency and certain rights kick in. The fine businessmen that own all these dumps around here know that, so they make sure you don't stay longer than twenty-eight days. They find a way to evict you.'

'But I've paid up for the entire month!' Aspen protested.

'So what? Who are you going to complain to? They'll come to you and say you didn't pay them enough, or you're a nuisance, or you've given the joint lice, or you're doing drugs, or you're a pimp, or whatever. They'll force you to leave, at gunpoint if necessary. Then they'll tell you — out of the goodness of their heart, of course — of a place you might want to try the next time you've got the cash, and you'll go there and take a room, and in twenty-eight days you're out again, and that landlord will recommend you to another of his friends. And so it goes.'

'Isn't that illegal?' Aspen asked.

'Sure. So's murder.'

But wouldn't it be sweet, the governor thought, *if those cops in the car over there were not waiting for any of us to do something, but preparing to bust one of the sharks who own buildings down here?* 'Nah,' he uttered aloud, shaking his head.

'What?' Aspen asked.

'Oh, nothing. Just be forewarned, is all.'

'Sounds like you've got experience in the matter.'

'Kid, experience is about all I do have.'

After a moment of quiet Aspen asked, 'You want some breakfast?'

'What?'

The younger man pulled a bag from his trouser pocket and opened it up to reveal almond cookies inside. 'There's a bakery a block over sells 'em a dozen for a buck. Seems like the best food deal down here.'

The governor nodded and took one, and from the corner of his eye, caught the police cruiser across the street beginning to move. It crawled past and then threw a U, and pulled up to the curb right beside them.

The policeman driving the cruiser got out and approached them. 'What are you fellows up to?' he asked.

'Why are you asking?' Aspen replied, but the governor shushed him by putting a hand on his arm.

'Up to nothing, officer,' the governor answered. 'Just eating cookies and wishing for milk.'

'Uh-huh. You live around here?'

'What is this?' Aspen said.

The governor squeezed the younger man's arm harder. 'Around, yeah," he told the officer.'

'Okay. Well, stay out of trouble.'

'Always do.'

The cop rushed back to the cruiser, and got in and pulled away.

'How can they do that?' Aspen asked indignantly. 'Treat us like we're criminals, like we've done something wrong. What gives them the right to hassle us like that?'

'Oh, I don't know . . . their uniforms, maybe? The fact that the courts are on their side?'

'Well, it's not right.'

'Son, you mind if I ask you a question?'

'Go ahead.'

The governor asked the question and Aspen's face fell.

'Hey, man, you're wrong about that.'

'I don't think so. You've put up an okay act, but you're not really one of us.'

'How'd you find out?' he asked.

'Remember after you found the body, and that detective looked at our hands? You talked about washing the blood and dirt off.'

'So?'

'So I've been out here for quite some time now, longer than I once thought was possible, and I've gotten to know an awful lot of folks out here with me. In my experience the last thing anyone living on Skid Row would think about is washing their hands. You want to know why?'

Aspen shrugged. 'You're going to tell me anyway, aren't you?'

'Mm-hmm. Because for all the time I've been here, I'll be damned if I could think of a place to go and do it. There aren't any public restrooms here. Hotels won't let you in if you don't flop there. Restaurants always claim their bathrooms are out of order. There aren't even any fountains anywhere.'

'Stores have got bottled water, don't they?' Aspen asked.

'Son, on any given day most of us are so damn thirsty that we drink anything we find that's liquid. Buy good water to pour over your hands? Down here no one in their right mind, and several that aren't, would do that. There's another sign you're a fake, too.'

'Yeah? What?'

'The way you get your back up any time you're getting questioned by a cop, like you're still paying taxes for their salaries. Down here, you don't get indignant.'

'Indignant? Kind of a fancy word for a bum, isn't it?'

The governor looked at him a long time, then said, 'Son, I may live on Skid Row, but I wasn't born on Skid Row. I learned a lot of fancy words when I was a young man. Anyway, if you want to live on the streets, and only the Lord knows why you do, you learn to treat the police with respect. And don't think it matters that you look like Mr. Wonderbread, all blond hair and blue-eyed. In fancy parts of the city, being a white boy might make a difference, but down here we're all the same color. Street color. Skid Row is the last American melting pot, and we've all melted together.'

'So just because I don't like cops much you think I'm a faker?'

The governor took a bite of the almond cookie and smiled as he chewed. 'Something else, too,' he said. 'In a place where people fight over food, you share it. Makes me want to love you, son, but if that doesn't prove you don't belong here, I don't know what does.'

'You share your money with others.'

'That's different.'

'How is it different?'

'What I do isn't your concern,' the governor snapped. 'I just want you to think about what I said and take care of yourself while you're here, before you go back to where you really belong.'

Aspen sighed. 'Has anyone else figured this out?'

'I haven't told anyone. I doubt anybody else cares. But I am curious why someone would willingly take up residence at the last station stop before oblivion. That's another fancy word, in case you missed it.'

'I'm doing research,' the young man said.

'For what?'

'I'd rather not say, though if I'm successful, it might bring awareness to the plight of the homeless in Los Angeles. It might make a difference.'

'If you say so. I'll see you later, son.'

'I'll walk with you, if you don't mind,' Aspen said.

As the two trudged down the street, a woman suddenly appeared out of an alley. Her hair was a mess, several front teeth were missing, and she was topless. She laughed lasciviously and called, 'I can give it to you, blondie . . . best y'ever had.'

The governor sighed. 'Come on, Lucy, the boy's off limits.'

'Go to hell!' Lucy cried.

'Can't, we're already here. C'mon now, there's cops out here. Go get some clothes on before you get arrested again.'

'Let 'em try!' she shouted.

'Yeah, let 'em try. Come along now, I'll find you something to wear.'

As gently as possible, the governor guided the woman back into the alley and the two of them disappeared from view.

He's definitely an interesting case, thought the young man who had not quite gotten used to thinking of himself as 'Aspen.' He was not even from Colorado, had never even been there, but *Aspen* was a lot better street tag than his real name.

Everyone here had secrets.

But having been made by a street guy, even one who seemed far more aware than the normal Skid Row bum, he realized his time on the street was most likely over. He'd already gotten what he needed after all.

The young man known as Aspen started back for his motel, and it wasn't a fleabag on Gladys Street like he'd told the old man they called the governor. That was just a ruse. His place was quite a bit nicer, since his employer was paying for it. He was particularly looking forward to a hot shower.

The dirt was the worst part of going undercover on Skid Row.

Even worse than the death.

5

Ramona Rios was normally not one to sleep late, but there seemed to be little reason to get up. Not today, not yesterday, not since she had managed to argue her way out of a job. Her first day of official unemployment had been spent not getting far from her phone, convinced that Robert Bauman was going to call and say it had all been a mistake, and please come back to work.

But that call had not come. Nor had any communication from the station's legal department, scheduling an exit meeting and discussing the termination of her contract. She had heard nothing, not from management, not from anyone on the crew, not from the other staffers.

Nor had there been any announcement about her leaving, nothing in the *Times*, nothing in *Variety*, nothing in *Broadcast and Cable*.

It was almost as though she had

imagined the entire incident, as if she hadn't worked at the station in the first place.

The only comforting word had come from her mother, who would have been justified in being upset by the situation since Ramona's loss of income directly affected her support as well. But all her mom had said was, '*Don't worry, Monita; the big jobs always come with big disappointments.*'

Gestating anger over her situation propelled her out of bed, just as it had all the days in the previous week. Ramona glanced at the digital clock on her dresser and read the time: 8:37 a.m. Once, she would have already been out in the field, made up and on camera live at this time. But that was then.

And it will be again, she thought.

Throwing her robe over her sheer night-gown (which she wore only for comfort, since there was no one else to appreciate it), Ramona stumbled through her apartment door and down to the lobby of her building to get her paper.

Nobody noticed her there either.

On the way back to her apartment, Ramona scanned the front page and saw the teaser at the bottom of the front page: *Henry expected to enter race.* The actual story was on B-1.

Great, Ramona thought, *they're finally holding a Puto of the Year contest.*

It was not until after she had finished her breakfast, showered, and dressed that she got around to reading the *California* section of the paper and found the article. Ramona could not keep from shaking her head as he read:

> *State Assemblyman and former actor Adam Henry is expected to announce today his candidacy for the office of Mayor of Los Angeles, at a press conference held in downtown this afternoon, sources close to the Assemblyman say. He is attempting to unseat Mayor Alberto Soto, who took office on a reform campaign in 2001 and is running for a second term.*
>
> *The decision to throw his hat into the already hotly-contested mayoral*

race was not unexpected, though Henry's office in recent weeks had been coy as to the Sherman Oaks' Democrat's intentions. 'Assemblyman Henry feels that he has been treated very, very well by Los Angeles, and he is anxious to give something back to the city,' says Kerry Stryker, spokeswoman for Henry's last campaign, who has remained an advisor to the 54-year-old relative newcomer to politics.

While Henry's political team is remaining quiet regarding future political ambitions, some observers see this decision to seek one of the nation's highest-profile municipal positions as the first step in a quest for the Governor's Mansion in Sacramento and, beyond that, national political recognition.

Isn't that just swell? Ramona Rios thought. With Henry as Mayor of L.A., nothing would stand in the way of people like Nick Cantone and keep them from consuming the heart of the city like a succubus. And there was nothing she could do about it. Not now.

Or was there?

Ramona suddenly went 'on point,' which was her own term for those moments when she suddenly saw a situation appear before her in total clarity, revealing itself in bright neon colors and Dolby sound. Was Cantone somehow involved in her dismissal from the station? Had she managed to step on the toes of the unofficial ruler of Los Angeles and gotten herself pushed out for it? She couldn't believe Bauman would stoop to such blatant intimidation from a member of the community, even an incredibly rich one, but Hulme was another story. Jason Hulme would eat out of someone's cat litter box if there was a way it would turn around and benefit him in the future. That had to be it. That had to be the answer. She had not been pressured to up and quit for insubordination. She had been forced out for asking too many tough questions of a man who had connections everywhere in the city, even, apparently, to newsrooms.

For the first time in a week, Ramona Rios felt really good. For the first time, she realized that she had lost her job for doing the right thing.

Not that she could make any of this stick in court. Ramona was not the egomaniac that some people made her out to be. She knew that she had ruffled feathers at KPAC. She also knew it was the only way to get ahead.

But what could she do now? She was off the air, and no one seemed to notice.

That was when the solution hit her, causing her to laugh out loud in her empty apartment.

No one noticed.

So for all anyone else knew, she was still working for KPAC!

Ramona scanned the newspaper article again for information regarding Henry's impending press conference, but found none. No matter; she had ways of finding out where it would be held. She still had plenty of contacts in the news business.

It took only two quick calls to get all the information she needed.

It came as no surprise to Ramona that

Henry's announcement was going to be made at the site of the press conference for Phoenix Terrace. She had been tipped off that the revitalization of blighted areas was going to be the centerpiece of Henry's campaign, which was no doubt being paid for by the people who would benefit financially from that revitalization.

★　★　★

Upon her arrival at the site, over which were crawling a couple dozen reporters, milling about in circles like so many scout ants, Ramona noticed that once again the location appeared to be free of any of the thousands of homeless who lived in the area. Looking around, she noticed that each corner of the block was being patrolled by a uniformed officer, which she first took to be LAPD. But upon closer inspection, even from a distance, the uniforms were not quite right, not regulation. Each team of men appeared to operate from cars parked on both sides of the street, and the cars were not police black-and-whites. It had to be a private security force.

Who's paying for this? Ramona wondered.

A small press check in table had been set up under a green parasol, and Ramona got in the line for it. A woman who had clearly once been a local beauty queen somewhere in America was checking names off the list. *Here goes*, Ramona thought, when it came her turn to approach the table.

'Hi,' the woman said with false cheer. 'Your name?'

'Rios, R-I-O-S.'

'Rios,' the woman repeated, looking over the list of names. Then she frowned. 'I don't seem to have you listed here.'

'Oh, Jeez, don't tell me they forgot again!' Ramona bluffed. 'This has to be an oversight.'

'Uh, the thing is, Ms. Rios, but I really can't let you in if you're not on the list.'

Ramona smiled. 'Who can I talk to about this?'

'Well, you see, the only person here right now is me, and . . . '

A voice came from behind her: 'Is there a problem, Ramona?'

She turned to see a blond, bearded stranger. Her mouth opened to say, *Do I know you?* but she stopped when she saw his slight smile, and one of his baby-blue eyes narrow at her. It was not quite a wink, nothing so obvious that could be seen by the check-in woman, but she took the gesture to mean *just play along.*

'Oh, hi,' she said cheerily. 'Yes, I have a problem. My name's not on the list.'

The man shook his head. 'I told them,' he said. 'Don't worry, I think we can straighten this out.' He stepped up to the desk and said, 'Ken Corder, *Hollywood Reporter*. My editor was supposed to put Ms. Rios on the list, too, but I guess they forgot.'

The woman checked the list and then said, 'Corder, you said?'

'Ken Corder, *Hollywood Reporter*. And yes, I know it rhymes. I've been told enough times.'

'I'm sorry, Mr. Corder, but I don't find your name either.'

'Oh, for . . . I'm going to kill Ozzie when I get back to the office! This isn't the first time he's screwed up like this.'

'Hey, can we move this along?' snapped

a man in line behind them.

'I don't believe this! But I guess there's nothing I can do, is there? Come on, Ramona, let's go back and have a talk with Ozzie.'

'Wait a minute,' she said. 'So he forgot to call in your name. When was the last time Adam Henry was covered in the *Hollywood Reporter*?'

Turning to the woman at the table, she added, 'Would Assemblyman Henry really turn down coverage on page one of a magazine everybody in his former industry reads because some assistant forgot to call in our names?'

'Ramona, I don't think — ' Corder began, but she ignored him.

Now growing wary of the long, and increasingly vocal line forming behind the two, the woman at the desk asked, 'Page one, you said?'

'This is major breaking news involving a movie star, isn't it? If that's not page one headline news, I don't know what is.'

'Look, Ramona, we need to talk . . . ' Corder said, trying to ease her away from the table.

'Let me ask you this,' Ramona said to the woman. 'Are you the one who will have to tell him and his campaign manager you turned us away?'

'Okay, here,' the woman said, handing him and Ramona stick-on press badges. 'Go ahead. Sorry.'

'Thank you.'

As they walked toward the press seating, Corder said, 'I can't believe you did that.'

'We're in, aren't we?' Ramona said. 'Now, Mr. Corder, but I have to ask . . . have we met?'

'No, and my name isn't really Ken Corder,' he said quietly. It's Danny Speakman."

'What is this about?'

'I'm a writer, and I'm working on an investigative piece about the plight of the homeless.'

'*The Hollywood Reporter* cares about the plight of the homeless?'

'No, that was just a bluff. I'm doing this on my own, but I want to sell it to a big publication like *The New Yorker* or *Vanity Fair*. I'm trying to get the real story of what goes on in places like Skid Row. I could come down here with my tape recorder and try to interview people, but I'm not really going to get their stories unless they think I'm one of them. For the last couple of weeks, I've been out here living on the streets like they do — trying to blend in.'

'I'm not sure it's working,' she said.

'Well, I'm not trying to blend in now,' Speakman declared. 'In fact, I spent an hour under the shower this morning to wash off the streets. And, truth be told, I was outed by this old guy down here they call the governor.'

'The governor?'

'Yeah, and it's a pretty good description because in a strange way he seems to be in charge of everybody. It's like he takes care of everyone else, but invisibly. Anyway, he saw through my cover but I don't think he's ratted me out to anyone else.'

'Okay, Danny Speakman,' Ramona said, 'I know you now, but how did you know who I was?'

'I've seen you on television. See, I've

only been out here in L.A. for a few months. I'm from the Bay Area, but during my stay here I've been reading papers and watching all the local TV channels for reportage on the homeless situation. I don't mind telling you there is precious little of it. But your live report last week, where you called out that developer, really impressed me. And you were right about the homeless being bused out, because I was on one of those buses myself. The reason I decided to bluff my way in here was, frankly, because I figured you'd be here and I wanted to meet you. I was rather surprised that your name wasn't on the press list, though.'

'Yeah, well, my bosses weren't as impressed by my report as you were,' she said. 'I was canned. I think the station management was leaned on by someone in the city. Wait, did you just say you were put on a bus and shipped out of Skid Row?'

'Yeah, or at least Aspen was. That's my street name.'

'Then you've got to come forward. You've got to make a statement and validate my report. Back me up. Then maybe I can file a wrongful termination suit.'

'I'd love to, Ramona, but I have to stay undercover, at least for a little while longer.'

'It looks like the circus is about to start,' she said. 'Henry's just arrived.'

She started toward the rows of folding chairs that had been set up to contain the members of the media, and Speakman followed her. Up at the podium, Adam Henry was getting fitted for a radio microphone. Smiling broadly, he was waving to the crowd, few of whom were waving back.

Once most of the reporters were seated, Henry began by asking, 'How are you all today? Thank you for coming out for this. I know all of you have busy schedules, so I appreciate it. And I don't want to take advantage of those busy schedules, so I will get right to the point. The city of Los Angeles, the city we love, is balancing on a teeter-totter even as we speak.'

He mimed the motion of a teeter-totter

going back and forth, which prompted a reporter seated behind Speakman and Ramona to comment, 'I wonder if he can do trapped-in-a-box or eat-peas-from-a-can, too?'

Ramona chuckled.

Henry held the pose for a few seconds, waiting for cameras to flash, instinctively knowing that this would be the shot that appeared in the newspapers, and then went on. 'Our fair city can either go down, becoming a place of greater crime, greater traffic congestion, greater inconvenience to our citizens and greater problems for our businesses, or it can go up. I would like to see it go up. I would like to see a reduction in crime. I would like to see more police officers on the streets protecting us. I would like to see a free and open environment for small businesses. I would like to see the city of Los Angeles thrive and become the envy of every other major metropolis in the country. It will never do that under the failed leadership of Alberto Soto. L.A. needs a real leader. I am therefore announcing my candidacy for mayor of the great city of Los Angeles.'

Henry paused for applause, but upon receiving barely enough to register, continued his announcement.

'I am willing to make this promise to the people of Los Angeles,' he proclaimed dramatically. 'If I am elected your mayor, I will do everything in my power to push this city into the twenty-first century by upgrading and modernizing the city itself. There are far too many areas like the one in which we are now standing, areas that have gone to seed, areas that are blighted and unsightly, areas that have failed to live up to any semblance of potential, areas that have been allowed to devolve into slums. There are too many areas such as this in the city of Los Angeles, and it is time we did something about it. This will be my first priority, fixing these terribly broken parts of an otherwise outstanding city. The development you see behind me is only the first of what I hope are many, many revitalization projects that will only improve and beautify Los Angeles here in the downtown district and elsewhere. If I am entrusted with the job of mayor, I will work each and every day of my term to foster this kind of revitalization,'

Henry offered to answer questions, and a dozen hands throughout the rows of seats shot up simultaneously. The questions those reporters shouted out were lowball to the point of being embarrassing.

'How much will your Hollywood career help you in your campaign?' asked a woman Ramona did not recognize.

'Is this the first step toward possibly running for national office?' inquired a youngish man who was also unfamiliar to her.

Jesus, they're plants! Ramona realized, surveying the group in front of her and realizing that all of the legitimate reporters who had their hands up were not being called upon. Some finally tried shouting out their questions, but these went ignored.

This entire thing has been staged! she thought, and then wondered why it surprised her. Ramona Rios had had enough. 'Give me some balance, Danny,' she said, standing up and putting a hand on his shoulder so she could climb up on top of her seat.

'What are you going to do?' he asked.

'Assemblyman Henry!' Ramona shouted at the top of her lungs, waving her free hand. 'Back here!'

Startled, Henry looked back at Ramona, and a frown crossed his face. 'What the hell are you doing here?' he muttered into the microphone. 'I was told they threw you out.'

At that, every reporter in the crowd turned around to see who he was referencing. Only then did Adam Henry realize what a blunder he had just committed.

'What did you say?' Ramona shouted back. 'Who told you I was thrown out of my job as a news reporter?'

Madeline Vega from KBNE television was two rows in front of Ramona. 'Is it true, Ramona?' she called back. 'Were you fired?'

'I am no longer at KPAC. But you didn't know that, did you, Maddy? None of you knew that.'

'Ms. Rios, I don't know what you think you are doing here, but — ' Henry shouted ineffectively.

Ramona ignored him. 'So how did he know? Who told him I had a confrontation with my station manager and left as a result? And why did he need to know that?'

Several of the reporters turned back to Henry and began asking just that, but Henry ignored their questions and motioned towards two security guards, who nodded and immediately started towards Ramona.

'They're not going to run us out of here, are they?' Speakman asked.

'I don't know,' Ramona replied, suddenly feeling frightened. The two guys coming toward her were coming fast and they were not smiling. She stepped down off the chair as the first one, an Hispanic with a shaved head who stood well over six feet and must have weighed in the range of two-fifty, started pushing his way past the reporters in Ramona's row, reaching for her. Ramona started speaking to him in Spanish, but she made no effort to run away. The man took her by the arm and yanked her toward him, nearly knocking her off of her feet.

'Hey, take it easy, jack!' Speakman shouted, trying to help her up.

By now the other reporters had abandoned their seats, and were scrambling for position to watch or videotape the altercation. Some were clambering over the folding chairs, and at least one had fallen or been pushed over them. Some of the faces looked frightened, others excited. As the Hispanic security guard pulled Ramona out of the crowd, the other guard, this one Caucasian but only slightly smaller, made a barrier with his arms to keep the other reporters away.

'What the hell are you thugs doing?' Speakman screamed.

'Our jobs!' the white guard shouted back, holding his beefy hand over a camera lens.

Over the commotion came Henry's nearly frantic voice calling for order and shouting, 'For God's sake, don't hurt her, just get her to shut up!'

'Are you telling a news reporter to shut up?' someone else yelled back.

'Well, she's been fired! She shouldn't be here!'

'How is it that you *do* know that, sir?'

another voice called. 'Who told you?'

'I . . . I . . . '

Realizing that the story was no longer the race for mayor of Los Angeles, Adam Henry slipped off the platform and dashed to his waiting limo. Several reporters followed him, still barking questions, while others remained in their seats.

They were not being paid to ask real questions.

Despite his age, Henry was still fit enough to outrun the members of the press with ease, though he did not bother to consider what it would look like on camera. All he wanted was to get away. Upon reaching the limo, he ordered the driver to get him out of there as quickly as possible.

As the limo disappeared down the street a siren announced the approach of a black-and-white police cruiser, which pulled up at the curb on Sixth, lights flashing, having appeared seemingly out of thin air. A plainclothesman and a uniformed officer got out and started jogging toward the commotion. Ramona did not recognize the plainclothesman as

Detective Darrell Knight, but Speakman did, having met him in his 'Aspen' persona.

He couldn't be recognized now.

Stepping back from the guards who were still holding onto Ramona, Speakman managed to drift back into the crowd until he was able to slip away completely.

Ramona, meanwhile, was shouting to the uniformed officer. 'I am being assaulted!' she cried.

A second cruiser now pulled up and two more uniforms got out.

Flashing his badge to the men holding Ramona, Knight said, 'Let her go . . . now.'

The two guards did, but they continued to glare at the much smaller detective in an intimidating way.

'Okay,' Knight said, 'anyone want to tell me what the hell is going on here?'

Ramona began. 'I'm a reporter and I was trying to get the attention of Assemblyman Henry to ask a question at this press conference — '

'You're not a reporter and you weren't

invited,' said the large Hispanic guard.

'Back off, tiny,' Knight said, returning the guard's withering glare. 'Of course she's a reporter, I see her all the time on Channel 8. Ramona Rios, right?'

'Yes, thank you,' she replied, smiling.

Knight then noticed that he was being filmed by anybody who had a camera. 'Shut those things off or lose 'em!' he shouted. 'You guys know better than that.'

The photographers complied, though most of them reluctantly so.

Flushed, almost shaking, Ramona went on with her testimony, including her meeting of Danny Speakman, whom she turned to bring into the conversation. Only then did she realize that he had gone.

'Wait, wait, wait,' Knight said. 'You're telling me that you met someone here who told you he was a writer working on a book who was posing as a bum for research? And the two of you simply bluffed your way in?'

'Yes, that's what he said.'

'Did anyone else see him?'

The other reporters had to admit that they had really not paid attention to the man seated next to Ramona.

'Is it important?' Ramona asked.

'It might be,' Knight answered casually. He was not about to let a pack of newshounds onto the fact that he was following the trail of a possible homeless serial killer, and someone — unknown — who was pretending to be a street bum, and who suddenly lams out when the authorities show up, had just made it to the Challenge Round of *Who Wants To Be A Prime Suspect?*

6

The howl that came from Nick Cantone's office was more extreme than usual. It froze his administrative assistant Delores in her tracks. She had heard him make a sound like that only once before, and that time it had been accompanied by the sound of a clock being thrown across the room against a wall, and the shattered pieces of it clattering to the ground. That tantrum had been prompted upon the news that a junior stockbroker at Smith Barney had mistakenly bought 100,000 shares of a stock that Cantone had intended to dump, costing him in the final accounting over two million dollars. It had also cost one of the local branch's partners, who happened to be the father of the junior stockbroker in question, his membership in L.A.'s exclusive Harrison Club which Cantone virtually ran.

Delores assumed that her boss's sudden rage had something to do with the call that had come in just a few minutes earlier from Devin Ronan, the city's District 16 councilmember, who was also Cantone's eyes and ears in L.A. government. Ronan called on average once a week, though this time, Delores did not even get the chance to put the call through to her boss's office. Ronan simply told her, 'Tell him to turn on Channel 5 and brace yourself,' before hanging up. Knowing that the plasma television in Cantone's office was almost always on and usually tuned in to Fox News Network, she relayed the message immediately. What followed was one minute of silence and then the explosion.

'*SonuvaBITCH!*' Cantone screamed, and Delores detected the sound of another hard object colliding with the wall. The developer then nearly tore his office door off its hinges and marched into the outer office. 'You'd think that Hollywood moron could do a *press conference* competently, wouldn't you?' he shouted.

Delores tried to keep the panic out of her voice as she replied, 'Yes sir, I would think so.' She had absolutely no idea what she was agreeing to, but knew that agreeing first and then gently raising questions later was the safest course.

'You'd think something as simple as declaring yourself a candidate for office could be accomplished without creating a frigging *riot*, wouldn't you?'

Ah, Delores thought, *we must be speaking of Adam Henry*. 'Yes sir, I would think so, absolutely.'

'*God!*' Cantone bellowed again, returning to his office. Delores desperately wanted to know what was being broadcast on the news, but she knew better than to walk into Cantone's office without being invited. So she sat it out, listening to the faint sound of the television and the occasional expletive. Finally Cantone reappeared. 'Do you believe this, Delores? I mean, do you frigging *believe* it?'

She shook her head. 'It's truly unbelievable, Mr. Cantone.'

Whatever *it* was.

He retreated once more to his office, stepped over the trash can that he had dropkicked, stepped over to his enormous mahogany desk, picked up the phone and jabbed in a number. The phone at the other end rang five times before the voice answered, 'Mr. Hulme's office.'

'This is Nick Cantone. Get him on the line. *NOW!*'

In the next second, though, he realized there was nothing Jason Hulme could do for him. Hulme had already lost control over the situation, and was therefore useless to him.

Cantone slammed down the receiver.

Whatever Ramona Rios was up to, and whoever she was really working for, simply being fired was not going to stop her.

It was time to call in a professional.

'Delores,' he called out, and his secretary rushed into his office.

'Yes, Mr. Cantone?'

'Take the afternoon off.'

The secretary was startled. 'Um, I still have a few more letters to transcribe — '

'It doesn't matter. You can do them tomorrow. Go on, go.'

'Yes, sir. See you tomorrow.' Rushing

back out, she quickly gathered up her purse and sweater, turned on the answering machine, and hustled out of the office feeling she had managed to dodge a bullet.

Once she was gone, Cantone unlocked the bottom drawer in his desk and withdrew a cell phone. Punching in a number, he waited five rings before a man answered.

'Hello, sir,' the voice said.

'Meet me at the club at 4:45.'

There was no point in asking the man whether or not he was available. He'd be there.

* * *

The Harrison Club was not identified by any signage on the street. One either knew what the three-story brick building tucked in between high rises in downtown L.A. was, or they didn't.

There were people in the city who were under the belief that the billionaire businessman's club no longer existed, which was fine with most of the

97

members. The Harrison was where Southern California's most affluent citizens, plus a few resident aliens, could meet to plan a deal, exchange funds, or hide a body, all while enjoying the best filet mignon or lobster to be found anywhere in the state.

Since Nick Cantone's guest was not a member, he was forced to enter through the secret guarded entrance that was accessible only from a private elevator in the back of an antiquarian bookshop located next to the club. Cantone had informed the guard his guest would be coming.

He, however, did not have to resort to any such subterfuge. He drove into the underground parking lot off of Flower Street and went straight to his reserved spot. A sensor on the concrete wall in front notified the staff inside that Cantone had arrived, which is why the club manager was waiting to greet him as soon as the elevator doors opened in the building's common area.

'Good evening, Mr. Cantone,' the manager said.

'Evening, George. Is my dining room ready?'

'Always, sir.'

Nick Cantone made his way up the wide, ornate, oaken staircase to the third floor, where three executive dining rooms were situated. They were mini-restaurants that were ready and waiting at all hours for their customers.

And if no customers happened to reserve on any given day, the five-star meals were simply deposited into the trash. One time a kitchen worker had once attempted to take some of the food with him and was caught. He was never seen again on the premises.

Cantone seated himself in the Calhoun room, the most intimate of the dining suites, and ordered a bottle of Lafite-Rothschild Bordeaux.

Both the wine and his guest arrived at the same time.

'Have a seat,' Cantone said, and the other man did, setting a leather satchel down beside him. 'Wine?'

'I'd prefer a scotch, Mr. Cantone,' Gunnar Fesche said, 'if that's all right.'

'Of course, of course.'

Cantone signaled for the waiter again and ordered a bottle of Dalmore, which arrived within seconds. Fesche sipped the liquor like he was tasting the nectar of the gods.

'Leave us now,' Cantone told the waiter. 'I'll signal for you when I need you.'

'Yes sir,' the waiter said, then hurried out.

'Now, then, Gunnar,' Cantone went on, 'we have something of a problem.'

'Your friend, the movie star?'

Cantone laughed mirthlessly. 'Problem doesn't begin to describe Adam Henry, but him I can handle myself. I'm talking about Ramona Rios.'

'Who's that?'

'A former reporter who turns up at all the wrong times, making all the wrong comments, and inciting all the wrong people to follow her leads into my affairs. She destroyed Adam Henry's announcement that he was running for mayor this morning, just like she turned the Phoenix Terrace press conference into a debacle. I will not have either Phoenix or the Henry campaign torpedoed, let alone by some beaner babe who thinks she's the L.A. Lois Lane.'

Fesche took another sip of his scotch. 'You want the ultimate package?'

'If that's what it takes, yes.'

'Do you have a photo of her?'

'I have better.'

Nick Cantone checked his Rolex and then pressed a small button on the side of the dining table. Instantly, the waiter entered the room. 'Albert, bring in a television, would you?'

'Yes sir.'

The waiter left again and returned a minute later with a television on a rolling cart. After plugging it in, he hooked it up to a cable access wire that was hanging on one paneled wall, and asked, 'What channel?'

'Channel 5,' Cantone said.

Taking the remote, the waiter selected the channel, and then passed the device to Cantone. The television popped to life. 'Will you be dining this evening, sir?' he asked.

Cantone turned to Fesche, who said, 'I had kind of a late lunch.'

'Some other time, then,' Cantone said. 'That will be all, then, Albert. I'll ring when I need you again.'

Once the waiter had gone, Cantone added, 'I'm not sure my stomach could handle dinner after watching this twice, anyway. I saw it earlier this afternoon, and there's no way they're not going to repeat it now. It's *news*.'

He pronounced the word as though he was describing a sickening body expulsion.

The five o'clock news came on and the two watched in silence for only a minute before the top local story appeared — the disastrous roll-out of the Henry campaign. It came complete with close-ups of Henry's befuddled expression as he attempted to grasp the situation and field unexpected questions, but was topped by shots of his running for his limo like he was on fire, with field reporters chasing him.

'God almighty,' Cantone sneered. 'Why didn't they put the *Benny Hill* music over this! My candidate. L.A.'s best hope!'

'Why don't you run for mayor yourself, Mr. Cantone?' Fesche asked.

Cantone snorted. 'I am not a public man, my friend. Neither would I care for a demotion. There, that's her, the dark-haired one with the mouth.'

'Quite a looker,' Fesche said.

'Feel free to make her less so, if you like.'

Cantone's hands tightened into fists as he watched the coverage being given to his puppet candidate's incompetence.

Fesche suddenly sat up straight. 'That blond guy next to her, who is he?'

'I have no idea. Why?'

Reaching down to get his satchel, Fesche said, 'Maybe I'm wrong, but I don't think so. That old black bum you asked me to keep a watch on, the one all the other bums look up to? The one you thought might be some kind of under-cover cop, trying to catch you shipping all the other good-for-nothings out of the area?'

'What about him?'

From his satchel, Fesche pulled a

couple 8 x 10 photographs and laid them on the table. 'The old dude I think is legit. I mean, he's really a bum, not a cop. But take a look at this guy.' He pointed out Aspen in the photograph. 'Clean him up a little, put some decent clothes on him, and you've got — '

'The man standing next to Ramona Rios at the press conference,' Cantone said. 'Good spotting, my friend. Check him out, too. Find out what he's up to, who he's working for. And if necessary . . . '

'It'll cost more.'

Nick Cantone smiled like a snake looking at a hamster.

'Gunnar, if you haven't learned by now that money is no object, you never will.'

7

It was nearly six o'clock before Ramona Rios got out of Parker Center, the downtown police headquarters. Detective Knight had held onto her until the two security guards had been released, just in case there was additional trouble. For Knight's taste, the guards enjoyed their jobs just a little bit too much, but since Ramona had opted not to press assault charges against them, there was nothing on which he could hold them. Like the soldiers they believed themselves to be, they gave little information except names, ranks, and information relating to the firm they worked for (some outfit based in Orange County called Monster Security). After a call to those offices to verify that they were correctly representing their employment, Knight sent them on their way.

Neither was Ramona charged with anything, since Knight was hard pressed to come up with any city ordinance that forbade one from impersonating an employed journalist. He cautioned her though that repeating such actions as she had taken that day could result in even more trouble, maybe even the accusation of stalking — a suggestion that first made Ramona swear out loud, and then laugh.

For her part, Ramona had actually been surprised by the questioning she had received from the detective. Most of it had pertained to Danny Speakman. She confessed that she had never met him before and had been more than a little annoyed by his sudden David Blaine disappearing act during the press conference. Most surprising was the fact that Knight had taken her to the police sketch artist to provide an official description of Speakman. She had asked what he was being suspected of, but of course the detective revealed nothing.

But she could not help wondering why, if the man really was a writer with a book deal, he would be so difficult to locate.

Just then Ramona realized she had answered her own question by using the word *if*.

Her news alarm was working overtime. If something was up regarding this guy Speakman, it was a story waiting to be uncovered.

By her.

And to hell with Channel 8.

Ramona had done her best to work with the police artist, watching as the talented woman interpreted her description. The first version was very close, though Ramona offered subtle corrections until the image was perfect. Every nuance of the face had been captured.

It was the best likeness of her ex, Lonnie, that Ramona had ever seen. And she hoped he got picked up, too.

As for Danny Speakman's face, she planned to keep that to herself, at least until she learned what he was really up to.

Announcing that she was free to go, Knight assigned a uniformed officer to walk out with her and drive her back to her car, which remained parked at the press conference site . . . if it hadn't been towed yet.

Outside of the station, Ramona was gratified to see that there were still a good

107

dozen reporters hanging around the back exit. One she recognized from the *Daily News*, and another two were from competing television stations. All shouted her name as though they were old friends and tried to shove microphones and tape recorders in her face.

Never having been on this side of a story before, she did not particularly care for the experience. The policeman tried to brush the reporters away but Ramona said, 'No, it's all right, officer, I'll talk to them. These are my *compadres*, after all.'

'I guess you know what you're doing,' he said, hanging back.

'Why did they keep you here so long, Ramona?' asked Suan Kim from Channel 2, whom she barely knew. Now it was 'Ramona' like they were classmates.

'I don't know, Suan,' she replied, 'maybe for my protection. If you're asking was I made uncomfortable during my time here, the answer is no, absolutely not.'

'So have you in fact been fired by KPAC?' asked another reporter, one she did not recognize.

'I was demoted to a lesser position within the news operation, which I had no intention of accepting,' Ramona.

'So you resigned?' Suan Kim asked.

'My position is that I was maneuvered into resigning. I had no intention of leaving my job otherwise. As to why I was backed up against the wall by management to the point where I felt leaving KPAC was my only viable option, you will have to ask Jason Hulme, the station manager.'

'Why did you show up today at the Henry press conference?' the reporter from the *Daily News* asked.

'Look, I might not have a home base at present, but I'm still a reporter like all of you. I felt there were questions that deserved to be put to Assemblyman Henry that were not being asked. But for now, the biggest question remains how Mr. Henry knew I was no longer at the station when no announcement had been made. Who told him, and why?'

'Who do *you* think it was Ramona?' Suan Kim asked.

'Maybe Jason Hulme can help you with

that,' she replied. 'And while you're asking him, you might also want to ask what he meant when he suggested I get on my knees in front of him, after which he suggested I could use my contract as a . . . as feminine protection.'

'Whoa!' an African American woman from Channel 7 shouted.

'And if he claims he never said that, ask who else was in the room who heard him.'

Even though Robert Bauman had done nothing in her defense, she was not quite ready to throw him under the bus as well.

'Now guys, you'll have to excuse me,' Ramona went on. 'I've had a pretty strange day and I'd like to go home.'

Turning to the uniform, who had faded into the background, Suan Kim said, 'Officer, is there anything you can add?'

'No ma'am,' the cop said, taking Ramona lightly by the arm and escorting her past the reporters. When they got to the cruiser, he asked, 'Where to?'

Ramona gave him the downtown cross streets, and then got in the back of the car.

The drive to Skid Row took place in

silence, broken occasionally by the squawk of the police radio. Remarkably, if not miraculously, her Mustang was right where she had left it — untouched, unticketed and untagged.

Seeing it intact made her happier than she would have thought possible.

Thanking the taciturn officer, Ramona got out of the cruiser and unlocked the door to the CRV, then waved back at the policeman who drove on. Once the black-and-white had turned the corner and disappeared up San Pedro Street, an elderly street man was on the sidewalk, having appeared out of nowhere as though he just beamed down from the Starship Enterprise.

'Heyyyyy, sister,' the old man said, giving her a toothless grin, 'I watched your car for ya. Made sure nobody messed wit' it. How 'bout some change?' He walked toward her and Ramona tensed. 'Kept it safe for you,' the street man said, holding out a filthy hand to her.

'I'm sure you did, but — ' she began, but then another man appeared on the other side of her, and this one's

111

appearance startled her even more.

'Here,' Danny Speakman said, slapping a five dollar bill onto the old homeless man's hand.

'Whoooo, God bless ya!' the man said, shoving it into his soiled pocket before anyone else had the chance to see it.

As he shuffled away from them, Speakman said, 'I was actually the one who kept an eye on your car.'

'You know, Mr. Speakman, you're like some roach, scurrying into and out of the light,' she said. 'And how did you know this was my car?'

'The vanity plate really isn't that hard to decipher.'

Ramona's plate read *ARRIOS*, an otherwise nonsensical Spanish word that phonetically turned into *R. RIOS*. 'Okay, I'll give you that one,' she said. 'Now would you mind explaining to me why you ran like Dracula from a cross earlier today, leaving me to deal with the police alone?'

'Oh, come off it, you loved it,' Speakman said. 'You loved the attention back there, and you probably relished getting pulled into the station. And clearly they did not arrest you, because you're here.'

'No, they did not arrest me, but they're sure interested in you, amigo.'

'In me?'

'Yes, and you haven't answered me. Why did you disappear?'

Danny Speakman sighed. 'Look, how about we go somewhere and talk this over, like maybe a restaurant?'

'You want to take me to dinner?' she said accusatorially, but in truth, Ramona was starving. She was also perfectly willing to have this man spring for a meal in return for his abandoning her.

'I will buy you dinner,' he said. 'Then we'll talk.'

Ramona gave him her best *but-you'd-better-watch-yourself-buster* look, before unlocking the Mustang and saying, 'Okay, get in.'

She suggested the Spence for dinner, an old wood-paneled steak house on Figueroa that boasted of never having closed its doors, even for earthquakes, for most of the 20th century. The place was crowded and noisy like usual and the aroma of searing meat permeated the dining area like a mist. The restaurant's walls were covered with old paintings and signage that were coated in a brown nicotine glaze still left from the days when smoking was allowed in public places.

'If this place is always open, when do they clean?' Speakman asked.

'You'd have to ask the county health department,' she replied, 'though since this place is owned by a former L.A. mayor, who is very, very rich, my guess is they're not that concerned about it.'

'You suspect everyone of something, don't you?'

'Don't you?'

'Sometimes.'

Ramona and Danny took a booth near the back. She immediately began looking over the menu, seeking out the most expensive item which appeared to be the prime rib. Since she did not particularly care for prime rib, she selected the tenderloin filet. Once the waiter, who appeared almost as old as the surroundings, had taken their order (and Speakman had given her a wry

grin when she announced her selection
— he was getting a sandwich), Ramona
started to laugh.

'What's so funny?' he asked.

'Oh, it's just been a hell of a week,' she
said. 'First, I get fired. Then I get
manhandled at a press conference for a
mayoral candidate. Then I get pulled in
by the cops. Now I'm on a date with a
homeless guy. It's just all hitting me.'

'This isn't exactly a date and I told you
I'm not really homeless,' Speakman said.

'Okay, I'm out with a fake homeless
guy,' Ramona giggled. 'I can't even get a
date with a real one.'

'It's symptomatic of an increasingly
strange world. But now that your mood is
clearly improving, maybe you could tell
me why you think the police were so
interested in me.'

'Sure, if you tell me why you were so
interested in staying away from them,' she
shot back.

'That one's easy, and innocent, too. I'd
already met the policeman who showed
up at the press conference once before,
only it was when I was in my bum

disguise. I didn't want him to recognize me from that and blow my cover.'

The waiter reappeared and placed a plate of French bread down on their table, and Ramona immediately took a slice and buttered it, then popped it into her mouth and chewed. 'That's really all there is to it?' she asked through the mouthful of bread.

'That's really all there is to it.'

'Okay. Now I feel even better about misleading them.' She described how she had dealt with the suspect sketch artist, which made Speakman laugh out loud.

'I hope I never get on your bad side,' he said.

The food then came and they spent the next few minutes simply eating in silence. The filet was the best Ramona had had in ages, though she ignored the flat, thick fries that came with it. The steak was nearly gone when she noticed Speakman watching her eat. 'What?' she asked, defensively.

'You seem unusually hungry, that's all,' he said.

'Latinas can't be hungry?'

'No, I mean you're eating like people I saw out on the streets, like you haven't eaten anything in quite some time, and might not again for a while.'

'Well, I did miss lunch, and . . . '

'And?'

'I guess I haven't been eating much in the past week.'

'Depressed over getting fired?'

'Technically I wasn't fired. Technically I quit, even though I was forced to. But yeah, you could say I'm bummed. No pun intended.'

'Are you having money problems?'

'Don't worry about me, okay?'

'All right, how about this . . . why did you get into the news business?'

'Why not?'

'Come on now, stop lobbing defensive answers back at me,' Speakman pressed.

'I suppose you wouldn't accept it's because it's what I wanted to do, would you?'

'There still has to be a reason.'

Ramona sighed. 'Okay, look, where I come from it's all about taking whatever opportunities are offered when they're offered. I started getting offers when I was thirteen years old, but they had nothing to do with journalism. I was developing, but not as a reporter. In middle school I joined the staff of the school newspaper because we often stayed late to turn out an issue. It was safe. By the time we were finished, everyone else was gone and I could walk home without being hassled by boys, and even a couple grown men. But I discovered I liked working on the paper. I liked finding things out about people. One time I even got in trouble for something I wrote. I hadn't brought drugs to school, or a weapon, or even dressed provocatively, like some of my friends did, but I still got threatened with a suspension . . . I'd learned about how our gym teacher was abusing kids and wrote it up without checking with our faculty advisor first. But damned if the gym teacher didn't quietly go on a sabbatical and not come back. That was when I learned the most powerful force in the world was truth.'

'So you became Ramona Rios, PI . . . which stands for paranoid idealist,' Speakman said.

Ramona was about to protest, but stopped. After thinking it over, she grinned and said, 'Maybe that should be the title of my autobiography. Anyway, I continued with journalism in high school and a year of community college. While I was there I managed to get some videotape of myself. My teacher told me that local stations were always on the lookout for minority reporters, and he even had a few contacts in town that I could approach. So here I am.'

'Maybe your teacher can help you rebound,' Speakman said.

She shook her head. 'He died not long ago. Cancer.'

'I'm sorry.'

'Why? You didn't know him.'

'No, but I don't like hearing about people dying. Like that bum I found dead in the alley. I didn't know him either but I hated to see him lying there murdered.'

Ramona snapped into reporter mode so quickly that she nearly dropped her fork. 'What bum lying murdered where?' she demanded loudly.

'Keep it down, okay?' he said, glancing

around. Nobody was even looking in their direction — not even the waiter. 'I stumbled on some guy's body down on Skid Row while I was in street man mode. He'd been stabbed.'

'When was this?'

'Five days ago.'

'How come I haven't heard about this before now?' she demanded.

'I can't answer that,' he replied. 'I'm not from here, remember? Maybe the murders of homeless people aren't reported in L.A., I don't know. You should have asked Detective Knight when you had the chance.'

'I didn't yet know about . . . ' A light went on inside Ramona's head. 'Wait a minute. Knight is the one handling the murder case?'

'I told you that. That's why I skipped when he showed up this afternoon.'

'You didn't say anything about murder, you only said that you had met him.'

'Oh. Well, I talked to him after I discovered the body. I guess Skid Row is his beat.'

'I think I should talk with him again,' Ramona said.

'If you do, see if you can find out exactly why he's interested in me.'

'I'll try. In the meantime, what are you going to do now?'

'Well, I was thinking of going back home and working on my article, but if the police need to talk to me some more about Jimmy's murder, maybe I should stick around in L.A. for a few more days.'

'Jimmy was the victim?'

'That's what the governor called him.'

'Do you know his last name?'

'No. Even the governor said he didn't know that.'

'Did the governor have any idea why someone would murder a homeless man?'

'Nothing specific, but from what I've been told it doesn't take much. Someone has food or a new pair of shoes, and someone else wants it, so . . . '

Ramona Rios shook her head, sending her dark tresses swaying back and forth. 'God, that sucks on so many different levels,' she said. 'How many pair of shoes and hamburger combos could be bought for the price of Phoenix Terrace? But Nick Cantone and the other rich *bastardos* who come into depressed areas and spend millions putting up monuments to their dirty names wouldn't spend a cent to help the homeless. Instead they want them gone.'

She stopped talking and stared off into the distance before repeating, 'They want them gone. Oh, my god, you don't think . . . '

'What, that developers are killing off the homeless instead of busing them out?' Speakman said. 'That seems pretty extreme.'

'I need to find out more about this Jimmy.'

'If you're planning on poking around on Skid Row, I can tell you first hand it won't be very pleasant,' he said.

'I'm not going to do it undercover, like you. I'm not that stupid. Oh . . . I'm sorry, I didn't mean that like it sounded.'

Speakman only smiled. 'It's all right. I understand it would be harder for a woman. Particularly an attractive woman.'

Ramona looked up at him and narrowed her eyes. 'Uh huh,' she uttered. 'I was wondering when you were going to make your move.'

'I'm not making a move,' he protested. 'I'm simply saying the women I've seen on the streets don't look like you. You'd never pass. And please don't try to tell me that you're unaware of your looks. Nobody on television is unaware of their looks.'

'All right, I'll accept your point.'

The waiter reappeared to take away any empty dishes, and Ramona asked for her leftover steak to be put into a container.

'Do you have a dog?' Speakman asked.

'No, but I also don't have a job at present,' she replied. 'I can't afford to waste food.'

After Speakman received the bill for the dinner, the two walked up to the upright cage by the front door that housed the cashier. Speakman handed over three twenties and took only a few ones in change back.

Outside on the street, people were queued up halfway down the block, waiting to get into the Spence.

'I love L.A. at night,' Ramona said, looking around at the illuminated buildings, standing like pillars of light against the blue-black sky. 'That's when it's at its best.'

To Speakman, the city at night looked like an experienced whore who puts on her finest jewelry to go out in the evening, knowing that the dark will obscure most of her hardness and age. 'You're smiling,' he told Ramona.

'Am I? Well, I like it here, that's all. Do you want me to drop you off at whatever five-star hotel you're calling home away from home?'

'Yeah, right. I'll walk and see the city at night, on your recommendation. Thanks, though.'

'You'll be okay?'

'I'll manage. Maybe I'll try to figure out your buses.'

'Good luck with that.' She held up her Styrofoam take-home container. 'Thanks for dinner.'

'How can I reach you if I need to?' he asked.

Ramona gave him her home phone number.

'All right. And if the next time you see me I look like a hard case on the streets, pretend you don't know otherwise, all right?'

'I'll do that,' she said. 'Though I am curious to see how you dirty down. Night.'

Ramona headed for her car at the small lot across the street from the restaurant.

Danny Speakman watched her until she got in and drove away.

Once she was gone, he pulled out a cell phone and punched in a number.

When he heard the voice on the other end, he said, 'It's me. I think our problem just got bigger.'

After explaining it to the man, he waited for instructions, which were slow in coming.

'All right, I'll keep an eye on her,' said the man who called himself Danny Speakman, Ken Corder, and Aspen, 'but I won't hit her. Hitting women is your specialty anyway.'

He lowered the cell phone, but could still hear the voice yelling: *Don't ever say that again! You understand?*

That made him grin.

8

The governor couldn't help but smile at the sight of a fellow homeless man across San Julian Street urinating on a soft drink advertisement painted onto the side of an abandoned store, while a pearl grey dove flew up over his head.

The sign of peace over a sign with piss, he thought.

Skid Row occasionally revealed its poetic side.

A police car suddenly appeared and screeched to a halt. There had been more police presence in the last week than the governor had seen in the last six months. For some reason, the cops had decided to take the murder of Jimmy very seriously.

An officer leapt out of the cruiser's shotgun seat and headed for the urinating man who, upon seeing him, unleashed another stream, this time of invective.

'You're breaking the law, sir,' shouted

the policeman, who looked barely out of his teens.

What happened to Velasquez? the governor wondered. Maybe he got promoted to an office job. Or maybe the worst happened to him. You just never knew.

The street man started shouting back, and waved his arms like a windmill. The governor saw the cop reach for his holster and decided he'd better get involved.

Before he could, though, he heard a voice call, 'Stand down, officer!'

Detective Knight was now heading across the street. 'Holster it, patrolman,' he said, flashing his badge.

The young officer straightened like a cadet and the street man finished fastening his pants, while glaring at the two of them with everything he had.

'He might have had a weapon, sir,' the junior officer protested.

'What's your name, officer?'

'Monroe, sir.'

'Monroe, the man had something in his hand, but I promise you it wasn't a weapon,' Knight said, which caused the street man to laugh raucously. 'I saw it, more's the pity.'

'He was still breaking the law, sir. Violation of code six-forty-seven.'

'Monroe, go on about your patrol. I'll deal with Whiz Kid, here.'

The uniformed officer turned and strode back to the car.

The detective waited until the cruiser had pulled away before turning to the homeless guy and saying, 'Use the back of a building from now on. No weenie-waving on the street. Now, beat it.'

The street man shouted something unintelligible, then shrugged, turned around and shuffled away.

After surveying the street in both directors, it took Knight only a few seconds to spot the governor. He started to walk toward him, calling, 'Sir, I'd like to speak with you.'

'Sir?' the governor said as the policeman approached. 'That's something.'

'Well, you didn't tell me your name the last time we talked, did you? You are one of the witnesses to finding that body, aren't you?'

'Old Jim? Yeah. As for my name, folks down here call me Governor.'

'What was your name before you were elected?'

The governor smiled. 'Sharlton Grosvenor.'

'Charlton? Like Heston?'

'No, with an S. Giving me that name was the worst thing my mama ever did to me, too. In the old days I used to go by Charlie. As for my last name, it looks like it should be *gross-venor*, but it's pronounced *grove-ner*. I think that's how I ended up getting elected, as you put it. Grosvenor sounds like governor when you're drunk or addled.'

'All right, Charlie.' From his pocket, Knight pulled out a folded sheet of paper, opened it and handed it to the street man. It was the composite sketch made from Ramona Rios's description. 'Seen this guy around?'

The governor studied the sketch, admiring the artist's skill. 'Nope, sorry,' he said. 'Never saw this man.'

He handed the paper back.

'Hang onto it,' Knight said. 'If you

think of it, show it around to some of the others down here. If anyone knows him, I'd appreciate it if you'd contact me.' After giving the governor a card, he shook his head and smiled. 'What am I doing?' the detective muttered. 'I'm so used to passing these things out to everyone I talk to, I didn't even consider you probably don't have access to a phone.'

'Oh, I think I might be able to find one if something's really important,' the governor told him, taking the card. 'What do you need this guy for?'

'Seems there's been somebody down here who doesn't belong here, somebody posing as a street guy, but he isn't really.'

'Is that a fact. What is he?'

'Some kind of journalist or writer. His name is Speakman, Danny Speakman.'

The governor frowned and looked at the sketch. 'And this is him?'

'We got a description of him from another journalist.'

'And you think he has something to do with the murder of Jimmy?'

'I don't know. All I know is a lot of things aren't adding up, and that's why I want to talk to this guy.'

'What's happened to ol' Jim anyway,' the governor asked. 'His body, I mean.'

'Officially he's still a John Doe, though we're calling him James Doe. We can't ID him. So far, his prints haven't turned up in any file. You'll contact me if you learn anything, right?'

'Yes sir.'

'Even if you suspect anything.'

'If it will help find Jimmy's killer,' the governor said. 'Hey, as long as you're here, did something happen to Officer Velasquez?'

'Yeah. He's in the hospital.'

'Damn. Wasn't in a shoot-out, was he?'

Detective Knight rolled his eyes. 'He was trying to install a room air conditioner at his home and fell off the ladder. Busted his leg. That's the story, anyway. Some of us think he took a dive to avoid working with his new partner. I'll tell him you send your regards.'

'Just say they're from the governor, though. No need to pass my real name on to him.'

'Do I need to worry that you're a

wanted man, and that's why you don't want your name revealed?'

'Detective, if any of us were wanted, we wouldn't be on Skid Row.'

'If you say so. Keep out of trouble, Governor.'

'Always.'

As Knight strode back to his car, the governor studied the drawing again. The part about someone who was pretending to be a real streeter seemed to fit what he had learned about Aspen, but even the worst artist in the world would not come up with this face based on hearing the man's description.

Something was going down on Skid Row, some mystery with a thousand pieces, all of which were swirling around like discarded papers in the wind.

As the governor stood thinking in the hot sun, a woman named Sally came up to him. She was rumored to once have been a television executive, but the governor wasn't sure he believed that. Then again, he wasn't sure he didn't.

'Hey, what happened to that movie?' she demanded.

'What movie, Sal?' the governor asked, pretending he didn't know.

A film company had come down last month to do location shooting, and after futile attempts to herd the homeless away, the producer opted to pay them as extras. The governor was assigned the roles of casting director and paymaster, handing out twenty dollars to each person who ended up in a scene.

'That was weeks ago, Sal,' he told the woman. 'They're long gone.'

'But I need more money. I need to buy things.'

'The mission can't help you with what you need?'

'They don't want me to come around anymore,' Sal said.

The governor doubted that was the truth, but arguing would be pointless. 'How much do you need?'

'Twenty dollars, like they paid before.'

'What are you going to use it for?'

Sally stared at the ground. 'It's that time.'

That's another thing nobody stops to think about when they talk about people living on the streets, the governor thought. Sure, there's no place to go to the bathroom, but for women, dealing with what his mama used to call *the curse* was as hard as finding a toilet.

'Look, Sally, I got a sawbuck on me, and you can have it if you really need it, but don't go spreading around that the First National Bank of Governor is open for business, you dig?'

'Yeah, yeah.'

Sal held out her filthy hand, which showed traces of old blood smears.

'Pull your hand back,' the governor said softly. 'I don't want anyone to see this transaction.' Reaching into his pocket he pulled out the crumpled ten dollar bill and slipped it to her.

'You're the last of the good ones,' Sally muttered, palming the bill. 'How'd the two of us end up like this anyway?'

'Life happens.'

'You mean shit happens.'

'Sometimes there's not much difference, Sal,' the governor said, turning and walking away, hoping he hadn't fallen for a fast line. She might be going off to buy a bottle of Red Lightning, a brand of popskull so toxic it also left red stains on the skin.

Her question *How'd the two of us end up like this anyway?* echoed inside his head. More and more lately, the fact that the governor was a fraud weighed on him. The only real difference between him and that kid Aspen, and apparently this Danny Speakman guy that the police were hunting, was motive for the fraudulent behavior, because like them he was not really homeless.

Nobody on the streets knew where he stayed at night. If anyone had ever stopped to wonder why the governor was never seen emerging from a pile of ragged blankets in a doorway, or a sagging cardboard box in an alley, or tucked into a corner of a mission or huddled on the walkway of the Second Street tunnel in the rain, they never asked about it.

There was little reason for them to, since on Skid Row people stayed where they stayed, and that was their problem. It took so much strength just to stay alive that worrying about somebody else was wasted effort.

For most.

Even so, the governor made a practice of glancing side to side with every step he took as he walked back home, to make certain that no one was following him with their eyes.

Home was a two-storey, red brick residential hotel, small — only eight units — stashed away on a block of Harlem Place between Main and Spring at the edge of Skid Row. The governor occupied half of the bottom floor, where two units had been combined. The place was kept up reasonably well, but not so well that someone driving by would wonder why it looked better than any of the neighboring buildings. And the rent was kept cheap, but that hardly mattered to the governor.

He didn't pay rent since he owned the building.

Sharlton 'Charlie' Grosvenor's story would have made a Column One in the *Times* if he'd allow it to.

He had grown up in Mobile, Alabama, did his stint in Nam, and after mustering out moved to Los Angeles to get into the music business. He had always played a mean guitar, but discovered he wasn't a mean enough person to turn pro. At least not enough of a cut-throat.

Instead he learned the art of short-order cooking and worked at a string of restaurants in the city, finally gaining enough support to try and open his own place, 'The Grove,' on Hoover, just up from 25th. He went into business with a couple of sharp yuppie types and offered the kind of food on which he'd been raised: ribs, barbecue, sweet potatoes and greens — what a decade earlier would have been called 'soul food.' For a while the place was successful. It was even written up in the papers. But then strange things started happening. The books be-gan not quite adding up, and by the time Grosvenor became concerned enough to pull his head out of the smoker and try to find out what was going on, his partners — each one with a powerful craving for nose candy, he would later learn — had vanished. So had the money required to keep The Grove open.

In fact, everything was gone, except the cans currently in the store room and the growing pile of bills, most of which he thought had already been paid.

Charlie Grosvenor was not the first to learn that the people to whom he owed money couldn't have cared less that he had been totally screwed by his trusted partners. He likened it to the demise of an old buddy from Nam, who had returned to the states in a box, but only with his top-half intact. *This is what it feels like to get your legs cut off*, he thought at the time. *They're there one minute and then* bam! *The next they're gone and you're not even sure how it happened.*

Charlie reacted to the sudden spiraling disaster the way so many had before him. He slid down the thin neck of a liquor bottle and splashed around in the dark wetness of despair. He lost the restaurant and before long, lost his home. What's more, the woman with whom he was living decided she wanted to go eat off of someone else's menu. Before Charlie even knew what was happening he was out on the streets living alongside the people he used to drive past and not think very much about.

He had been on Skid Row for nearly five years when the reprieve came.

It happened at the end of a particularly bad week, even for a streeter, in which he had been beaten up by a much larger man over half a bottle of Everclear. Having a couple bucks in his shoe that his assailant didn't find, he had made his way to a market to buy something that would dull the pain in his ribs and jaw. Instead his attention was attracted by a new Lotto sign behind the counter. He was suddenly struck by the only possible way out of his situation.

It was insane to even think it would work, but it was the only particle of light in his life at that moment. So Charlie Grosvenor bought a Lotto ticket.

And lost.

But he bought another one the next week.

He lost again.

He bought a third and a fourth and a fifth one.

He lost, lost, lost.

Yet it remained a particle of light. With

each failed ticket, he thought ever harder about what he would do with the money if he ever won anything. He could not get his head around the revenge of living well, and not being particularly religious, he did not plan to tithe it all to a church. God never got any of that money anyway, only his advance men. Playing the 'If-I-Won-the-Lotto' game for Charlie always came up with the same mental response: he would use whatever money fell his way in the wind to help others on the street. Like him, many of these people did nothing to warrant their desperate situation. They were victims of circumstances, too, playing a sloppily-dealt hand against a society that held all the aces.

To ensure he had enough to buy his weekly Lotto ticket, Charlie stopped drinking anything harder than a Burger King root beer. He bought ticket after ticket after ticket.

And racked up loss after loss after loss.

He skipped one week, giving his two dollars instead to a woman with a small child, both of whom looked like they had not eaten in a week. But the next week he bought two tickets.

And lost.

And a ticket the week after that.

And lost.

And one the week after that.

That was when Sharlton Grosvenor won 8.6-million dollars.

Once the shock abated, he ran to the Midnight Mission and stayed in one of their hot showers until he was forced to get out. He got a haircut and shaved his beard, and took the best suit of clothes he could find that fit his lanky body, in order to look good enough to accept his check from the California Lottery.

On a whim, he asked one of the mission's cooks if he could borrow an apron, which he wore over his clothing at the check ceremony, explaining that he planned to use the money to open a new restaurant. He gave his real name to the press, but that was one of the last times he ever used it. It was also why he was so cautious about revealing it now. In the long run, though, it didn't matter. What people remembered, if anyone remembered his winning at all, was the Guy in the Apron, not someone named Sharlton Grosvenor.

For the next year he lived a double life, spending his days back on Skid Row, helping people out as subtly as he could, while retiring each evening to a plain but pleasant apartment not far from his bank branch. He contacted a financial advisor who had no idea of his daytime activities or persona, and then set about buying a few residential buildings in the downtown area that no one else seemed to want, and began offering units dirt cheap to people who wanted to escape living in the other kind of dirt.

Eventually he moved into one of them himself.

Charlie also paid for classes for those who wanted to take them, to help get them off the streets, but always through a foundation he had set up rather than in person. He did not want anyone on Skid Row knowing who he was, or what he was worth.

The only luxury he permitted himself out of his deal was to buy a good Gibson guitar. He learned his old, creased fingers were still able to make the strings sing when he wanted them to. (Though his frequent spicy chicken dinners at TiJacques', the Haitian restaurant on Fifth and Main that he had invested in after a devastating fire from faulty wiring threatened to shutter the place, could also be considered luxuries.)

When Charlie Grosvenor arrived at his building, he went in through a normally-locked back door, looking around to make certain no one saw him. The ghost act was hard to keep up, particularly when the two young boys who lived in the building were playing outside, but he managed.

Opening the door of his suite, he noticed that he had forgotten to turn off the DVD player after watching a film last night. 'Damn,' he muttered to no one.

Six or seven million bucks left in the bank still didn't mean he needed to be wasting electricity. Every streeter could eat lunch for the cost of the juice he'd just squandered through carelessness.

After turning it off, he went to the kitchen and he grabbed some milk from the fridge, then opened a fresh package of Nutter Butters. He gobbled down a half-dozen of the cookies with a swig of moo juice. Then he went to his bathroom and peeled off his clothes, dumping them in the special hamper that contained his 'work' outfits. He had four identical, or nearly so, sets of clothes, all kept in varying states of dirtiness and disrepair, but none of which were so reeking as to pollute the air in his rooms.

When he needed to wash up, like when he had to visit the offices of his attorney or financial planner, he could easily do it, and then explain away his sudden cleanliness to the others on the row in a variety of ways — if they asked. Most didn't.

As long as the governor was ready with a dead president, either coined or printed, most did not care if he looked scrubbed or not. He was, however, glad that he had not done a wash-up in the days prior to Detective Knight's asking to see his hands.

Since today's errand was not as official as visiting an office, he had planned only to spray off the top layers of grime. But once he got under the shower, Charlie didn't want to leave. He ended up doing the full wash, wax, and detail, including shampooing his hair and beard for the first time in a month.

After the shower he dried his hair and brushed it into an acceptable style, and then worked to shape his long, full beard. When he was finished, he looked a little bit like the comedian Dick Gregory.

Putting on some fresh underwear (which was yet another luxury because nothing in his life as a millionaire meant more to him than clean Jockeys anytime he wanted them), he reached into a tiny closet for a pair of khaki slacks and a deep blue dress shirt. After slipping into a pair of loafers, he angled a Panama hat over his semi-tamed hair, put on an expensive pair of sun-shades. Tucking his wallet into his back pocket, he ventured out again.

No one seeing him would recognize him as the governor.

Charlie wanted to find out more about this Danny Speakman, who, according to the detective, was some kind of writer or reporter. And if someone worked in the print trade legitimately, there was one place where they could be traced.

9

Even though the central branch of the Los Angeles Public Library had become dwarfed by the skyscrapers that had grown up around it, it remained an impressive-looking building. The new wings that were constructed after two devastating fires in the 1980s took away the original building's symmetry, but he loved the mosaic pyramidal cap on top of its tower, and all its exterior carvings and engravings. The pyramid was a fitting image since the building's interior was laid out like a pharaoh's tomb, with long escalators taking the place of shafts rising up and down between chambers, old murals covering the ceilings like early 20th-century hieroglyphics, and even sphinx statues flanking a grand staircase that was no longer the main access from floor to floor.

A long time ago Charlie had read that the middle name of the library's architect was 'Grosvenor,' though he doubted they were related.

Rather than walk to the downtown landmark, Charlie had taken a bus.

At times, he worried he was spoiling himself.

The lunch hour was wrapping up when he got there but the library courtyard, a tiny square of nature amidst a world of concrete, steel, and glass, was still dotted with workers from the surrounding office buildings eating their brown-bag meals or poking into takeout containers. There were several streeters as well — none begging for food, but simply appreciating a place to sit, if not lie down. Going through the enormous doors of the structure, Charlie nodded to the security guard, who said, 'Hello, sir.' Normally his first stop during a library visit was to go up and gaze at the murals which represented the history of California . . . at least the Eurocentric history that was widely accepted in the 1930s when they were painted. He loved the murals. They were old and faded and wore a dark patina of grime from decades of exposure. A little like him.

On this day, though, he went straight to the Tom Bradley Wing, which was named after the former mayor of Los Angeles, where the computer lab was located. Anyone with a library card could log onto the Web for thirty minutes.

Charlie had thought about getting a computer of his own many times before. He never did so, however, because he remembered somebody at a bank one time telling him that once you put your name on the Internet, you forfeit any semblance of privacy. Whether that was true or not he didn't know, but it was enough of a caution to cause him to fear that his presence on the Web might somehow lead to discovery of his secret.

Luckily, there was no line of people waiting for a computer, so he had to cool his heels for only five minutes before a terminal opened up.

A self-taught typist, Charlie Grosvenor was a hunter-and-pecker, and he had never fully mastered using the mouse, so a couple precious minutes of his half-hour were wasted getting accidentally shuttled into unfamiliar screens. Finally he made his way back to the homepage, where he typed in the name *Danny Speakman*. Of the five pages that popped up, representing three different Danny Speakmans as near as he could figure, none indicated any relation to a writer or journalist.

Next he tried a bookselling site to see if Danny Speakman had any books published, and came up with nothing. Then he realized that 'Danny' was likely a nickname. Charlie tried a general search for *Daniel Speakman*, but again came up with nothing.

The mystery of Danny Speakman was deepening.

He was about to give up when a voice just behind him whispered, 'I can't find him, either.' Startled, Charlie turned around to see a strikingly beautiful Latina's face hovering inches from his own.

'You shouldn't sneak up on people like that, young lady,' Charlie said.

'Sorry.'

'If you're waiting for the computer, I still have about twenty minutes left.'

'No, it's not that. I'm Ramona Rios. I

used to be on the television news.'

'Okay.'

'And you're the one they call the governor, right?'

'They who?'

'People on the street. The homeless. I've been following you, and — '

Now Charlie Grosvenor was alarmed. 'You've been what?' he cried, unable to keep his voice down.

'You were pointed out to me this morning by a bagman, and I followed you to an apartment. I thought about knocking on the door and forcing a meeting, but instead I waited. I saw you come out looking like this, different. Then I followed you and got on the bus behind you.'

'Damn, girl. Since you say I look different from the street man you followed to an apartment, how do you know I'm him?'

'Your walk is the same,' she said. 'You hold your head higher than other homeless people.'

'Who said I was homeless?'

Ramona smiled. 'You did.'

Charlie looked at her skeptically.

'You just asked me about the street man

I followed to your apartment, but I never said I *followed* a street man, I only said you were *pointed out* by a street man. All I said was that I followed a man known as the governor. You identified yourself as a bum.'

'That's not a term I like very much, young lady,' Charlie said. 'Unless you're talking about a baseball team. I prefer the word streeter.'

'Sorry, but you *are* the governor, aren't you?'

Charlie sighed. 'Yeah. And I hope you're on my side.'

'I am, believe me. I'm looking for Danny, too. I ran into him just a few days ago and he spun me a story about posing as a bu . . . a streeter for an article he was writing.'

A young man approached them and said, 'If you're done with that computer and just going to talk instead, can I get on it?'

'If the only thing you're looking for is Danny Speakman, then you're done,' Ramona told Charlie. 'I promise that you won't find him.'

'All right.'

Charlie Grosvenor logged off and got up from the chair.

'Let's go to the café,' Ramona said, walking ahead of him to the escalator, which took them to the main level.

Located near the Flower Street entrance, the Book Ends Café was rarely full, so getting a table was easy. Charlie planned on ordering nothing more than an orange juice, but the Chinese food chain that was part of the café smelled so good, he ended up adding a plate of vegetable egg rolls onto the bill. Ramona ordered a cup of tea which she sweetened with honey, and a fruit bowl. At the cash register, Charlie pulled out a twenty and said, 'My treat.'

Ramona started to laugh loudly.

'What's so funny?' Charlie asked.

I can't even get a date with a real home-less guy, she remembered telling Danny at dinner the night before. Now she had one.

'I'll tell you later,' she said. 'It's personal.'

They carried their trays to a table by the window and sat down.

153

'I'm willing to bet you're not going to tell me why you have money and live in an apartment while only pretending to be a bum, are you?' she asked.

If you really were willing to bet, you might know, Charlie thought, but simply said, 'And you'd win. The truth is, I'd appreciate you not telling anyone else where I live and what you've seen me do today. I'm not doing anything illegal, if that's what you're thinking, but I do have my reasons for continuing to play the part of a streeter. Which I was for a long time, by the way.'

'At least tell me what should I call you,' she said. 'The governor sounds too official.'

'Call me Charlie. Just Charlie is fine if I can call you Ramona.'

'Please. So, why are you looking for Danny Speakman?'

'You first.'

'Because I like to know who I'm dealing with.' She gave a brief recount of their meeting at the press conference, and his disappearance when the police arrived. 'Call it reporter's instinct if you want. Your turn now.'

'The police are looking for him in connection with the murder of a fellow I knew on Skid Row.'

'Oh, my god. How do they think he's involved?'

'They don't know. I think they want to talk to him because he doesn't really belong on the streets, so that makes him a person of interest. But I can't really figure this thing out, because there's another kid on the street who doesn't belong there, either. He calls himself Aspen, like the town in Colorado, and he claims to be doing research for something, but he won't tell me what.'

'Research. Like for a magazine article, maybe?'

'I don't know. He wouldn't say.'

'Could the guy you know as Aspen and the one I know as Danny be the same guy?'

Charlie shook his head. 'The detective on the case showed me a sketch of Speakman, and it looked nothing like Aspen. Besides, the detective already met Aspen because he discovered one of the bodies.'

'Oh, god,' Ramona said, as a half-dozen disparate facts all came together in her mind like a multi-car collision. 'Is Aspen by any chance tall, well-built, blond, and blue-eyed?'

'Yeaaaaah,' Charlie drawled. 'But he wasn't the guy in that sketch.'

'I'm starting to think that was the dumbest thing I've ever done,' she said, going on to explain the trick she had pulled on the police and the sketch artist.

'I don't know about all you've done, Ramona,' Charlie said, dipping a hot egg roll into sweet-and-sour sauce, 'but I'd have to agree with you. That was pretty damn dumb.'

'It seemed funny at the time, and we'd just broken up . . . why am I trying to defend myself? It was dumb. What do you know about Aspen?'

'I didn't even know the boy's name was Danny Speakman, or that he was a journalist. You seem to be the one who knows him.'

'For what it's worth, he likes you,' she said. 'He mentioned you to me. That's why I sought you out.'

'And followed me across downtown L.A.'

'Danny doesn't know anything about that. I did that on my own initiative. I am an investigative reporter, you know.'

'Maybe you should be investigating why anyone would want to murder ol' Jim,' Charlie said.

'Fine. I will. With your help.'

'My help?'

'Look, if what Danny said is true, you know everybody down there. You're one of them. At least you let people think you are.'

'Honey, if you think you can trick me into letting you in on my secret, you can forget it. But I don't want you investigating me, so I'll tell you this much. I'm now in a position to help those down on the row. I wasn't always, Lord knows, but I am now. You don't need to know how. The thing is, I don't believe in the approach the politicians like to throw around, that trickle-down business where the money's all supposed to rain down from the top. What I believe in is the bubble-up system where you help the people from the bottom, and hope they start to rise up on their own. And if they can't, for whatever reason, at least you've done something to make their lives just a little bit easier.'

'The streetwise Socialist, that's you,' she replied.

'Label it whatever you want. I don't care about labels except those on cans of beans or tinned meat.' Charlie dunked another egg roll into sauce and popped it into his mouth.

'Would you mind if I ask your opinion of the Phoenix Terrace project?' Ramona asked.

Once he had swallowed, Charlie said, 'That thing they're planning to build on Skid Row? Well, look, Ramona, somebody's going to spend a ton of money to put that sucker up, and when it's done, it's not going to help a single person who lives down there. In fact, we'll probably all be gone. The money people are only going to want the well-offs living there, and the well-offs aren't going to want to be reminded that they're spending a fortune to live on Skid Row. I don't yet know how they're planning on getting rid of all of us, but you can bet they're planning it.'

'Oh, lord,' Ramona uttered.

'What's wrong?'

'Do you think it's possible that the death of the street man is an example of the way the developers are planning to get rid of all of you?'

As possible as a homeless black man winning millions in the lotto, Charlie thought.

'I sure hope not,' he said. 'Though it is funny how that detective keeps coming around. Streeters have turned up dead in the past, but then the cops would show up, take 'em away, and that was that. But Knight is actually working the case. What does that imply to you?'

'Maybe that Jimmy is, or was, somebody important?' Ramona offered.

'Or maybe he wasn't the only one who was murdered. Maybe there's been more bodies that turned up. Do you have any contacts in the police department, being a reporter, and all?'

'I have some contacts who have

contacts,' she replied. 'What do you want me to find out?'

'Any information they might have discovered about Jim. Don't let on that we suspect there's some kind of serial killer running around on the row.'

'I can look into that. What do you plan to do?'

'Well, see if anybody knows anything more about Jimmy, I guess. And if I happen to run into Aspen in the process, I'll definitely try to find out what he's up to. How can I get in touch with you?'

Ramona pulled out a business card and wrote her cell phone number on the back. 'Very few people have this number,' she said, 'so I'd appreciate you protecting it.'

Charlie nodded and asked, 'You got another one of those?'

Ramona handed him a second card, and taking her pen, he wrote a number on the back. 'That's my home number. I don't have a cell. There's a machine on it where you can leave messages if I'm not there, which I probably won't be.' Before handing it back to her, he held it up. 'If you could memorize this number and then destroy this card, I'd appreciate it.'

'All right.'

Charlie rose and carried his tray to the trashcan, where he dumped the disposables before setting it on top. Ramona followed him.

'Since I parked my car by your apartment,' she said, 'I have to take the bus back with you.'

'Actually, I think I'm going to walk back. Walk off those egg rolls. Since you pointed out that you recognized me by my gait, all I have to do is change it.'

Charlie stooped himself over a little and took slower steps.

'All right. Thanks for lunch.'

'Keep in touch.'

They exited the library.

The man who had been sitting on a bench outside of the café pretending to read a book, who had ridden on the same bus with them to the library, watched them leave. After a few seconds, he left the book on the bench, got up, and casually followed.

At Flower Street they split up, each going in a different direction. That hardly mattered, since the old jig, whoever he was, was of no concern to him.

Gunnar Fesche's focus was solely on the woman. She was the one to be tailed. She was the one to be silenced.

10

The governor was back on the street within two hours and looking far better than usual.

He also had a new sense of purpose, one that went beyond his usual goal of trying to help the people around him without being caught at it.

He felt it was up to him to figure out exactly what had happened to Jimmy Doe because he knew the streets in ways no policeman or reporter ever could.

'Whoa,' the street man who called himself Calvin shouted to him.

Calvin was probably under fifty, though his tanned face was lined from squinting in the bright sunlight, and his thick, sweeping hair (which looked like it was stolen from a 19th century president) was steely gray. Calvin claimed to have been a standup comedian before hitting bottom, and who knew? Maybe he had been.

'What happened to you, man?' asked

Calvin, who wore a heavy, soiled trench coat even in ninety degree heat.

'What do you mean?' the governor replied.

'You look like you're going out on a date, bro. You run through a carwash or somethin'?'

'I got my quarterly delousing at the mission, if you must know,' the governor lied. 'New set of used clothes, too. Should be good for another year. Maybe you should go there, the Corpus Christi Mission on San Pedro. Get a hot shower and a meal.'

'Nahhhh,' Calvin drawled. 'I don't like those places that feed you so much Jesus you don't have any room left for the Spam.'

'Can't force you to go, but it's there. I used to go there sometime with Jimmy.'

'Little Jimmy? With the wonky eye?'

'Yeah.'

'Haven't seen him in a while.'

'You won't see him again, either. He's dead.'

'No shit.'

'Stabbed. A new kid found him in an

alley. Kid called Aspen.'

'I don't know any Aspen.'

'How well did you know Jimmy?'

'As well as I know anybody, I guess,' Calvin said. 'Why're you asking?'

This is what the governor had been wary of, coming off like an interrogator. *Play it cool and casual*, he thought.

'I'd like to find out who he is, is all. He's down on Mission Road listed as John Doe, and that's the way he'll stay until someone can identify him. I think he at least deserves to have a name even though it won't do him no good anymore.'

'A name,' the other man muttered. Then he shouted: 'Calvin Bennett Glore!'

'What?'

'Calvin Bennett Glore. That's me. That's my name. If something happens to me, now you know. Calvin Bennett Glore. Used to work under the name Cal Bennett. Cal Bennett tonight at The Improv. Did television, too, till I had to take a powder.'

Calvin started laughing uproariously revealing a toothless grin.

'Had to take a white powder! Mounds of it! Had to have it. We all did back then. That's the way television worked. Book a show, have some blow. Say a line, do a line. Snort the powder, read it louder. Now you're broke, steal your coke. When the lines go away, Dad, you're dead in L.A.'

Calvin laughed again.

The governor hoped this wasn't his club act.

'Jimmy was one of them, you know,' Calvin went on.

'Them who?'

'Bibley people. Selling God — like there really was some big, damn, bearded bozo up there who really gave a crap about anyone down here. I'm going to tell you something, Governor. If there really is a God, and he allows people to live the way we do without doing anything about it to help us, then he'd better find another line of work cause he sucks big, green ones at being God.'

The governor was in no mood to argue one way or the other, but he was puzzled. He had been around Jimmy for years and had never heard him spout the gospel. 'Why do you say he was . . . what did you call it . . , Bibley?'

''Cause he had a damn Bible!' Calvin shouted. 'He found out I was a performer and he asked me if I'd read it to him. He said he was having problems with his good eye, too, and it was getting hard for him to read, but if I was used to delivering lines, I'd be good at it. I told him to go to hell, that the only jokes I tell are the ones I write myself.'

'That was perhaps a little harsh,' the governor said, gently.

'It was perhaps a little true,' Calvin replied. 'I told him to ask God to read it to him himself, since he'd know how to pronounce all the names. Then I threw the book back at him. He acted like I'd thrown a Ming vase, and actually dove to catch it like some little pocket Bible was the most valuable thing in the world. Then he went away. Say, Governor, all this talking's made me thirsty. You got any extra on you I could have?'

'For some bottled water, you mean?'

Calvin laughed like he'd heard the

world's funniest joke.

'I think I got something, hold on.'

Charlie reached into his pocket, and then said, 'Aw, dang . . . my cash was in the pants I left at the mission when I got these new clothes. They probably burnt it by now.'

'Ohhh . . . !' Calvin wailed. 'How stupid can you be, man?'

'Memory starts goin' by my age. You'll find out.'

After slurring a bouquet of epithets, Calvin lurched away and went down the street, shouting at nothing.

Maybe he'll actually go to the mission to look for it, the governor thought, knowing he wouldn't find anything. The whole story of the mission was, of course, a lie. The truth was Charlie Grosvenor had shoved a roll of singles in his pocket before leaving his apartment, a few of which he easily could have peeled off for Calvin Bennett Glore, aka Cal Bennett.

But he hadn't liked the guy's act well enough to buy him drinks.

Charlie stopped worrying about the one-time comedian and instead turned his thoughts to Jimmy's Bible. If Calvin's description of Jim's reaction to its having been cavalierly thrown around was accurate, that book held great importance for the little man. Or else it held something inside. Maybe Jimmy had stuck money between the pages and used it for a bank. But if that was the case, he wouldn't have asked someone to go through and read it to him. And Calvin had likely been right again by assessing it as a giveaway. Complete Bibles were handed out on the row like candidate buttons at a campaign rally. A streeter might have a hard time convincing someone to stake them a Big Mac combo, but you could always acquire a holy book.

So what made this particular one of Jimmy's so important?

'There was personal information in it,' Charlie told himself.

Surely somebody on Skid Row knew Jimmy well enough to know where he bunked at night, whether it was in a flop house, a mission, a tent or just a box somewhere. He had to find out who, but he had to do it without inspiring suspicion in people who were already prone to paranoia.

Charlie tried to think, quickly concluding his brain worked a little better in the shade. Stepping around to the lee side of a run-down storefront church on Sixth Street, he sat in the relative cool and forced his brain to work in uncharted areas.

Where had he seen Jimmy most frequently?

The mission, but that didn't mean he squatted near there.

Who had he seen Jimmy with most often?

Charlie admitted to himself he had never really kept track. Jimmy was simply one among many down here who he considered his charges.

If Jimmy really was, as Calvin had put it, 'Bibley,' was there anyone else on the row similarly religious?

Charlie had rarely heard the word 'God' on the streets without 'damn,' or something worse, following.

This Sherlock Homeless stuff isn't as easy as it sounds, he thought, and then laughed at his own joke.

And a moment later, it hit him.

He had been approaching things from the wrong direction. The question he should be asking himself is why Jimmy's body was found where it was. Was there a significance to that alley for the little man?

Charlie headed out through the hot sun to the place where Aspen had found Jimmy, passing only a few streeters, huddled like piles of old laundry in doorways. Cars crept by on Sixth Street (traffic made zooming impossible in downtown L.A.), their drivers working hard to keep from looking at the people on the sidewalks or shuffling across the street sometimes against the light. When he got to the alley, he turned into it and began to inspect it, finding little but piles of trash. It looked no different from when Jimmy's body had been found days ago.

He kept walking, going deeper into the alley.

Then he discovered what he had never known existed.

At the end of the alley was a vacant lot,

impossible to see from the street entrance, which was a virtual campground of large cardboard boxes and ratty one-person tents. Had Jimmy lived in one of these? Had he been killed while trying to protect his 'home' and property? Both were certainly possible.

But how had he missed the fact that this hidden 'neighborhood' existed?

'You gettin' too damn old for this,' he muttered to himself.

As he approached the homesteads, he noticed several pairs of feet sticking out from them. The ones that had metal carts or empty baby carriages shoved up against them were most likely uninhabited at present. A small dog emerged from one box, looked warily at Charlie, but then wagged his tail and ran to him when he knelt down. Scratching and petting the dog was probably going to load both he and his fresh clothes with fleas, but what the hell? He'd had fleas before. He had a means of washing them away; the pooch didn't.

'Hey, boy, how you doin?' he asked, as the dog, which appeared to be a mix of all breeds at once, happily lapped up his attention.

A voice from inside the box hollered, 'Hey! Who took my dog?'

'He's out here,' the governor called back.

A long-bearded man with a combat jacket and Brillo-pad hair slithered out and confronted him. 'What're you doin' with my dog?'

'Just petting him, is all.'

'That's my dog.'

'He looks like a good one.'

'He's mine.'

'Fine,' the governor said, standing up, which caused the dog to run in a circle and beg for more attention. *Pooch deserves better*, he thought. 'I'm looking for someone who knew Jimmy.'

'Jimmy who?' Brillo-head asked.

'Don't know. That's one of the things I'm trying to find out. He was a little guy with a bad eye.'

'He's not here.'

'I know. He's dead.'

Brillo-head looked at the governor for a long moment, then muttered, 'Guess that's why he left all his stuff.'

'What stuff would that be?'

'What's it to you? It's mine now. He won't need it. He left it.'

'Was there a Bible in the stuff he left?'

'Yeah. So what?'

'So mind if I see it?'

'It's mine now,' Brillo-head said.

'Do you read it?'

'No. I tear out pages and stuff them into the bottom of my shoes. Makes 'em more comfortable.'

The governor approached the man, and the dog stayed with him. 'I'll buy that book, or what's left of it, from you.'

'With what?'

Glancing around to make sure he was not being watched, the governor pulled his roll of ones out of his pocket, and Brillo-head dove for it. Expecting something like this, the governor side-stepped him and watched the dog run out of the way as the man fell to all fours.

'Ow, dammit!' Brillo-head cried.

'Five of these are yours, my friend, no fighting, no argument, if you go get me that book,' the governor said. 'Tell you what else. I'll give you another five for the pooch.'

The dog wagged his tail as though he understood.

'You're a crazy mufu,' Brillo-head said.

'Probably. And you're ten bucks richer if you go get me that Holy Bible and let me take this fleabag off your hands.'

'Havin' that dog by me got more money,' the man said.

Whether that was actually true or not, the governor knew that there was a widespread belief having an animal increased the proceeds from begging.

'Let me ask this, then,' the governor said. 'How fast can you run?'

'What the hell you talkin' about,' Brillo-head said, slowly, painfully getting off his knees.

'What I said. You think you can outrun me? Or this dog?'

'My foot's bad,' the guy said.

'Well, if I take off, I'll bet you another five this dog follows right behind me,' the governor said. 'We only just met, but it looks like we kinda like each other. So I can split right now with pooch here running right after me, and you're left with nothing, or you can take the ten and give me the good book. Either way, the dog's going with me.'

'You said you'd bet another five to find out.'

The governor sighed and peeled another five bills, then when he saw movement out of the corner of his eye, shoved the wad back into his pocket.

He folded the fifteen singles into a square and palmed them.

'Go get the Bible,' he said.

Turning around, Brillo-head shuffled back to his box and returned with a small, beat-up, leather-bound book about the size of a paperback novel. Once the governor had it, he handed over the cash.

'Pleasure doin' business with you,' he told the guy.

'Yeah, yeah, come again sometime. As for that dog, he don't like beer.'

Jesus, Charlie Grosvenor thought, *the poor thing's probably dehydrated.* 'There's a free clinic on Central,' he called back to Brillo-head. 'If your foot's that bad, go down there and have it checked.' Then looking down at the dog, he said, 'Come on, pooch.' It dutifully followed him.

It was an exceedingly rare day that Charlie spent more time in his apartment than on the streets, but he had work to do, so he returned home. The first thing he did was set down a big bowl of water, which the dog lapped dry in no time. Then he took some hamburger from his fridge and quickly fried it up, and set it down on the floor. Charlie suspected Pooch — that was the dog's official name now — was near starving, but he hoped it wouldn't get too used to people food.

When the dog was sated, Charlie led him into the bathroom and put him in the tub. Since he had washed his hair this morning the shampoo bottle was still on the edge of the bathtub. After wetting the dog down, which it didn't seem to mind, he slathered the shampoo all over it and lathered it up watching hundreds of dead fleas get washed off in the rinse. He soaped Pooch up once more and carefully rinsed him again, then dried him off as best he could with one of his bath towels.

After a couple of wet shakes, Pooch

looked like a new man. Though God only knew what kind of dog he was.

Taking up the Bible, Charlie went into the small living room, sat down on the couch, and turned on the floor light next to it. Pooch leapt up beside him, uninvited, and stretched out with his chin on Charlie's leg.

'What the hell am I going to do with you?' Charlie asked, smiling as he stroked the dog's head.

Pooch thumped his tail on the sofa, sounding as if he were tapping out Morse code, but Charlie couldn't translate it.

11

As Ramona Rios hung up the phone, she made a mental note to never do anything for Bree Whitcombe again. The Channel 9 field reporter, who called Ramona for advice her first week on the job, after her news director had made unwanted advances, had contacts all through the police department, but refused to share any of them. 'You know I can't break my confidences,' Bree told her over the phone. 'Sorry, Ramona. But we should get together for lunch sometime.'

Yeah, sure, Ramona thought.

She wondered if the governor was having any better luck.

Ramona was on the verge of calling Robert Bauman, her former news director, and playing the *You-owe-me-this!* card when her phone rang. She answered it immediately.

'Is this Ramona Rios?' a man's voice said.

'Yes, who is this?'

'FTD delivery. I have some flowers for you.'

'Flowers? From who?'

'The name on the card is Lonnie DeMarco.'

Lonnie! So her ex was attempting to apologize to her?

More likely, this was the opening salvo in his attempt to wheedle his way back into her life.

'Ma'am?' the voice said.

'Is it an expensive bouquet?' Ramona asked.

'Yes.'

Part of her wanted to refuse them as a way of telling Lonnie to stay in hell.

But why waste good flowers?

'Can I come in?' the voice said.

'Yes, come on. Bring them to apartment two-nineteen.' She then hit the buzzer to open the front door of the building.

Two minutes later, there was a knock on the door of her apartment, and Ramona pulled it open.

Her ex, Lonnie, was standing there in person, with no flowers.

'You bas — ' she managed to get out before he forced his way inside. 'Get out of here or I'll call the police.'

'Oh, you don't have to,' Lonnie sneered. 'They're my new friends. I've spent all morning with them attempting to convince them I'm not somebody named Danny Speakman who's stalking homeless people.'

In spite of herself, Ramona started to giggle.

'You think this is funny, do you?'

'Well, yeah. I take it you were able to exonerate yourself.'

'Yes, and the cops were able to verify that I've been out of town for the past two weeks. I just got back yesterday, and today, this.'

'You have to admit, it was a really great sketch.'

'Oh, yeah, it's brilliant!' Lonnie shouted. 'It was so good, when I went to pick up my mail at the post office this morning I was recognized. The cops thought I knew something about some murder, and then they told me that a witness had given my description to the artist, and then one of them happened to let slip that the witness was a television reporter. Well, gee . . . who could that have possibly been?'

Ramona Rios laughed again.

'You're insane, you know that?' Lonnie said. 'You've finally gone over the edge. And the cops aren't very happy with you, either, because of your little joke. You're probably going to be hearing from them.'

'Actually, I'd kind of like to talk with them again. I have some questions for the detective.'

'Everything's just a game with you, isn't it? Everything always has been.'

'Oh, and phony flower delivery isn't a game?'

'Would you have opened the door if I said it was me?'

'No, which is why you had to lie your way in. Standard operational procedure for you.'

'Oh, gimme a break!' Lonnie shouted. 'You want to know why I went elsewhere? I was tired of being an assistant!'

'What are you talking about?'

'Everything's about you, Ramona, only you. Our entire relationship was about you.'

'As I recall, you did pretty well for yourself.'

'I'm not talking about the sex. I can get sex anywhere.'

Ramona rolled her eyes so violently it hurt.

'I'm talking about *us*,' Lonnie went on. 'You never had time for me. Anything I wanted or needed had to wait because you were too busy being the queen of TV news reporters. But you're not on the air anymore. You get dumped by your station, too?'

'As I recall it, I was the one who threw you out.'

'I was going to leave anyway.'

You can't fire me, I quit! she thought, grimly. The new recurring motif of her life.

'Lonnie, I just don't have the energy for this,' Ramona sighed. 'You want to pretend that breaking up was your idea, fine. I just don't care anymore. Can you understand that?'

'I understand you put me through the day from hell today.'

'You want me to apologize? Okay, I

183

apologize. What I did was pretty dumb. Happy?'

'If I thought you meant it, I would be,' Lonnie grumbled.

'Then go somewhere else to find your happiness,' Ramona said. 'Go, Lonnie. Get out.'

He started to walk toward her door, then stopped and turned.

'For whatever it's worth, Mona, I do appreciate your apology,' he said. 'I didn't think you had it in you.'

'Great. Send me some real damn flowers some time and we'll call it even.'

Lonnie DeMarco left without another word, and she closed the door behind him, genuinely not knowing whether she ever hoped to see him again. This at least had been a little bit of a closure. Bumpy closure, but closure. And while she savored the idea that he'd been sweated by the cops for a while, with no harm, no foul, she was increasingly aware that her little stunt with the sketch artist had been pretty foolish. Maybe dangerously so.

The best course of action seemed to be to go see Detective Knight, come clean, and admit her deception, and then give an accurate description of Danny Speakman to the police artist, and hope she was believed this time.

Since she wanted to talk to the police anyway, this was a good excuse to do so.

After putting herself together, Ramona headed out, taking the elevator down to the parking garage underneath her building. She walked toward her car, stopping only at the sound of a projectile ricocheting off of a concrete support pylon an inch from her head, spraying dust and chips past her.

She heard a muffled pop and instantly the window of a car, not hers, exploded beside her. Instinctively, Ramona dropped to the concrete floor between two cars. 'Who are you?' she screamed, her voice echoing throughout the concrete garage.

She didn't really expect him to answer.

No more shots came.

Ramona remained on the filthy, greasy floor for ten minutes. No other shots had been fired. The shooter had fled. Whoever it was must have concluded they were taking too much of a chance to keep firing at her, even with a silencer. And they had to be using a silencer, otherwise the sound of the shot itself would have been deafening in the garage.

But why the hell was the person firing at her in the first place?

When Ramona felt it was safe enough to rise to her feet, she did so, and ran to her own, blipping it unlocked. It took several tries to get the key in the ignition, she was shaking so badly.

Over the years people had pointed out to Ramona that she was lethal behind the wheel, but this time it was justified. She roared out of her parking spot, narrowly missing the front fender of a car parked across the way, and sped to the electric eye beam that opened the garage from the inside, waiting impatiently for it to lift. Her tires squealed as though in terror as she shot out of the garage and onto the street.

Outside, Gunnar Fesche sat behind the wheel of his Miata and watched the Rios woman drive past like a bat out of hell. He had blown the opportunity and put the woman on her guard, and he was not looking forward to reporting back to Cantone about his failure.

But then, why would he have to?

Cantone had told him to call and confirm that the job was done, not keep him updated on failed attempts. There was no doubt the job *would* be done, and soon. The lucky Latina's good fortune wouldn't hold out forever. The next time, he'd make sure he found a spot with better lighting.

Fesche got out the car and went back to the garage's heavy security door, which he had easily picked open, and strode back in to look for the bullets. There was no sense leaving souvenirs for the cops. The one that had struck the car window was easy to find; it was laying on the driver's seat, waiting for him, practically calling his name. The one that had ricocheted took longer to locate; by using mental geometry, he charted its probable path and found that it had rolled under one of the cars.

Let Rios go ahead and file a police report. It would be her word against the lack of evidence.

Fesche crept back out of the garage and went to his car, already thinking about Plan B.

There was always the flower delivery pretense, Fesche thought, if she wasn't too savvy to fall for that one.

Then again, women were women, and flowers were flowers . . .

12

'You don't believe me?' Ramona Rios shouted at Detective Darrell Knight. 'You think I'm making up someone taking a couple shots at me?'

'You haven't exactly been the most forthcoming of witnesses, you know,' the detective replied. 'In fact, you're lucky I'm not holding you on an obstruction charge for that cute little stunt of yours regarding the suspect description.'

'I was on my way down here to make good on that when I was fired upon.'

'Did you see anyone with a gun?'

'No, but — '

'Did you hear a gunshot?'

'A gunshot?'

'You know, a loud *bang*?'

'I *know* what a gunshot sounds like, and no, there was no loud bang. I think the guy was using a silencer.'

'I thought you said you didn't see anyone.'

'I didn't!'

'Then how do you know it was a guy?'

'I . . . I just assumed it was. But one bullet pinged off of a concrete pylon and the other hit a car window and shattered it. And then I heard footsteps running away.'

'All right, Ms. Rios,' Knight said. 'Why do you think anyone would want to take a shot at you?'

'I don't know. I did a story on school shootings not long ago. Maybe the NRA is after me.'

'Or maybe it's good publicity to make people believe they are.'

'What are you saying?'

'I'm saying you're not offering me any real evidence to go on. You didn't see a shooter, you didn't see a gun. Maybe it was a kid with a pellet gun, or even a slingshot.'

'So you're going to do nothing?' she said.

Detective Knight exhaled loudly. 'All right. Give me your address.'

Ramona did so and Knight picked up the phone on his desk and punched a button. 'Betty, would you connect me to the desk sergeant at Wilshire division?' he asked. After a few moments of rubbing his forehead, he said, 'Hi, who is this? Sergeant Welbeck, this is Detective Darrell Knight, Central division, and I have a report of possible gunshots fired this evening in the parking garage of an apartment building at Twenty-nine Seventeen South Victoria Avenue. Could you ask a team to check it out, please? Tell them they should see the apartment manager.'

'No, I don't know his name,' Knight said, and looked to Ramona.

'Ralph Scranton, and he's a drunk,' she said.

'Ralph Scranton is the manager's name, and for what it's worth, he may be inebriated. Have them look for any evidence that a shooting of any kind occurred. Right, of any kind. Thanks.'

'Should I be there?' Ramona asked after Knight had hung up.

Knight shook his head. 'If they find any traces of bullets, you can talk to them and fill out a report. But since you've admitted to falsifying your earlier testimony, you're going to see our sketch artist one more time, and this time you're going to describe the real Speakman.'

'After which you'll arrest me for obstruction?'

'Don't tempt me,' Knight sighed, knowing he wouldn't. As a deputy chief once told him, throwing a reporter in jail was like eating Dodger Dogs at the ballpark. It's satisfying at the time, but it will come back to haunt you later.

As Knight led Ramona through the station to the office of the sketch artist, she asked, 'So what have you learned about the homeless guy who was killed on the street?'

'Why should I tell you anything?'

'I'll take that as 'nothing.' You haven't learned a thing.'

'Pretty sure of that, are you?'

'Pretty, because if you had learned something about him, like his identity, you'd enjoy not telling me what you know. You'd say something cornball like 'That's for us to know and you to find out.' Instead you're deflecting the question altogether.'

'Have you ever thought of joining the force?' Knight asked.

'Never. Why?'

'Because I have sergeants who couldn't have figured that out.'

'I like what I do,' Ramona said, but she couldn't help smiling.

'We have no ID, no motive, no suspects, nothing except your friend Speakman, who is a person of interest.'

When they went into the small workspace of the artist, whose name was Marilyn Yee, she recognized Ramona. 'We're doing this again?' she asked.

'We're doing it again,' Knight said, 'only this time with accuracy.'

'You've never criticized my work before.'

'And I'm not now, Marilyn. We were both misled. Get to work, Ms. Rios.'

This time Ramona gave a perfect description right down to the shade of Speakman's blue eyes, which were rendered in the drawing as medium gray.

'This is a bit different,' Marilyn said.

'Yeah, sorry,' Ramona muttered. 'Make the eyebrows a little thicker and darker. They really made his eyes stand out.'

When the drawing was finished, Detective Knight walked Ramona back to his desk. 'If it comes out that you've played us again, Ms. Rios, you're mine.'

'I haven't, I swear.'

'Then you can go. If the local officers are still at your place, give them my best regards.'

'And if they prove I was telling you the truth, I'll be sure to call.'

'Do that.'

Ramona strode out of the station and back to her car, only to be stopped by another man. She started to yell, and the fellow looked at her with a puzzled expression. He was tall, dressed in a dark suit, and wore his black hair in a buzz-cut.

'Ms. Rios?' he said, his voice whispery.

'Yes, do I know you?'

The man flashed a badge.

He was FBI.

'I'm sorry if I startled you just now,' he said.

'I'm a little jumpy tonight. What can I do for you, Agent . . . '

'Fleer. Michael Fleer. Is there somewhere we can talk?'

'I'm on my way home,' she said. 'I was shot at tonight.'

Turning an intense gaze on her, he finally said, 'That's not good.'

'Tell me. It was in the parking garage of my apartment.'

'And you're going back?'

'There are police there, looking around.'

'Perhaps I should come with you,' the agent said.

'What is this about?' she asked. 'How did you know me?'

'We know of you, Ms. Rios. I'm afraid you've gotten yourself mixed up in a very dangerous business with some very dangerous people. I'd feel safer if I could follow you home.'

'Like a stray dog, huh?'

The man didn't laugh. Ramona studied his handsome face and saw nothing to distrust. She couldn't help thinking she had seen him somewhere before, but having generic looks was probably an asset for a Fed.

'All right, go ahead and follow. Though I presume you already know where I live, being a G-man.'

She slid into the passenger seat of her Ford Escort as he jogged to a black Audi parked a half-block away, and got in.

A few times on the way to her building, Ramona thought she had lost him, only to see the Audi reappear in her rearview mirror a few moments later.

As they neared her apartment building, Ramona saw that two police vehicles were pulled up outside, their lights flashing. A group of inquisitive neighborhood people had gathered to watch from the sidewalk. Glancing in the mirror, she saw Agent Fleer motioning her to keep going, even as he parallel parked on the street. Ramona pulled around to the driveway and saw that the garage door was fixed in an open position, and a group of officers were inside, along with the building manager.

'Go talk to them,' Fleer said, opening the car door. 'I'll stay back. Local police don't always appreciate bureau agents showing up unannounced.'

Ramona drove in slowly and pulled into her spot. One of the officers went up to her car.

'Ma'am, I'm going to have to ask you to pull out again,' he told her.

'But I'm Ramona Rios,' she said, getting out of the car. 'I'm the one who called this in.'

'The call we got, ma'am, was from Detective Knight at Central division,' replied the policeman, whose nametag ID'd him as Treacher. He was very young and very white.

'I was with Detective Knight when he called. I was seeing him on another matter. I live here, and I'm the one who was fired upon.'

'Then you deal with this, because I'm tired of this crap,' the manager shouted. 'I don't need the police hanging around for no reason.'

'It wasn't for no reason, Mr. Scranton.'

'Actually, ma'am,' Officer Treacher said, 'we've been over the garage and we can't find any evidence that a shooting took place. No bullets, no shell casings, nobody else heard anything.'

'What about the broken car window?'

'That could have been shattered by anything: a club, a crowbar, a screwdriver even.'

'So I'm lying?'

'I'm sorry, ma'am, but we just can't find any evidence to support a shooter. If you want to file a report anyway, we can do that.'

'Why bother?' Ramona said, pivoting on her heel and marching toward the open door.

'Ma'am, your car?' Treacher called after her.

'How do you know my car's really there?' she said angrily. 'Maybe it's just a figment of my imagination, like the shooting!'

Outside, Michael Fleer was waiting for her.

'I could have used some help in there, you know,' she fumed.

'It was best I stayed back,' he replied. 'In my experience, local police don't always appreciate bureau personnel showing up unannounced.'

'They didn't believe me.'

'Because of the acoustics in the garage I could hear what that officer was saying. You know, Ms. Rios, maybe you should at least consider the possibility that it really was a kid with a pellet gun.'

'Hey, you were the one who said I'd opened up some box of trouble.'

'All right. Let's go up to your apartment and talk there,' Fleer said, and Ramona looked at him somewhat skeptically.

'You still don't trust me?' he went on. 'I suppose that's good, in a way.' Then the agent took his gun from the shoulder holster under his coat and handed it to her. 'Now you're the one in power.'

She hesitated for a few moments, then took the gun from him. 'You might have another one,' she said.

'I might, but I don't.'

Sliding the gun into her purse, she led Michael Fleer inside the building and to the elevator, watching through the glass as the police officers got into their cruisers, turned off the lights, and pulled away. The crowd of lookie-loos outside began to disperse.

After riding up in silence, Ramona went to her apartment and unlocked the door, letting him in. Ramona tossed her purse on the counter separating the kitchen from the living room, something she did habitually, not even thinking about the gun tucked inside it.

'Can I offer you something?' she asked.

'I'm fine,' Fleer replied, looking around.

'Mind if I get something for me?'

'It's your place.'

She went to the fridge and pulled out a diet Dr. Pepper, then motioned for Fleer to take a seat on the sofa, while she sat in a chair across from him.

Then it hit her.

'Now I know why you look familiar,' she said.

'You think I look familiar?'

'Yeah. You ever watch a TV show called *Angel*?'

'No.'

'The lead actor looks like you. I interviewed him once. David somebody. Your hair's shorter, and your eyes a little darker, but other than that you're a good match.'

'Hmm. If the bureau ever tires of me, I guess I could seek a job as his stand-in,' Fleer said.

'All right, Mr. Federal Man, why don't you tell me what is going on. What sort of trouble have I tripped over? I'll bet it has something to do with the Phoenix Terrace development, doesn't it?'

'That's part of it.'

'What's the rest?'

Agent Fleer leaned forward. 'Ms. Rios — '

'Call me Ramona.'

'Very well, Ramona. The corridors of power in Los Angeles are a dark and dangerous maze. It's not easy to find your way through them. You mentioned Phoenix Terrace, but that is only the tip of the iceberg. What do you know about — '

Her phone rang then, drowning out his soft, sanded voice.

'Oh, god,' Ramona said, 'that's probably Detective Knight calling to give me hell because the cops found nothing in the garage. Hold on.'

She grabbed the phone and greeted the caller, then said, 'What? Are you kidding? Really? Oh, hell. I'll be right down, okay?' After hanging up Ramona turned to Fleer. 'This is so bizarre. I had a fight with my ex-boyfriend tonight. It was the fight we never had when we split up. I kinda got on his case about not sending me flowers because he pretended to be a flower delivery guy to get inside the building. So now the jerk sent me real flowers, and the guy's downstairs. I'll be back in a second.'

'Ramona, wait,' Fleer called, but she was already out the door and into the hallway. A neighbor was getting out of the elevator, which she managed to catch before the doors closed. She could hear Michael Fleer calling her name but ignored him, punching the button for the first floor.

In the lobby she could see someone outside the door holding a huge floral bouquet.

'You're an ass, DeMarco,' she muttered to herself, 'but I accept your apology.'

Ramona opened the door.

'Are you Ramona Rios?' the delivery man asked.

'Yes. And these are from Lonnie DeMarco, right?' she said.

'Wrong,' the man responded, brandishing an automatic with a silencer.

13

The soft thump of the pocket Bible falling off of Charlie Grosvenor's lap awakened him. It made Pooch stir as well.

Pooch's head was still on his leg, which was probably what had made him fall asleep in the first place. There was something about holding onto a sleeping creature that was contagious, or at least as best Charlie could remember from his limited contact with the baby that Yvonne had told him was his — the child he hadn't seen in more than thirty years.

The dog's tail started to wag when Charlie moved. 'You probably need to go out, don't you?' he asked, receiving more wags in response. Getting up and going into the kitchen, Charlie got a plastic baggie from a drawer and then took Pooch out back. He wasn't worried about the dog being unleashed. Having found home, Pooch wasn't going to go anywhere else.

After sniffing around the tiny back yard, and spending a good amount of time on the trash cans, Pooch found himself a spot on the grass and took care of business. When he was done, Charlie picked up the substantial pile with the baggie, and muttered, 'Damn, dog, what'd you eat?' Knotting the baggie closed, he dropped it in one of the cans and then the two returned to his apartment. He made a mental note to price out one of those dog doors with the flap, so Pooch could come and go as needed.

Going to his hallway closet, Charlie pulled out two clean towels and carried them into the living room, where he carefully set them down on the floor. 'Okay, boy, those are yours,' he said. 'That's your bed, at least until we can find a better one.' Pooch examined the towels, then stood on them and circled five or six times, after which he dropped down and curled up, and then let out a long, satisfied dog sigh.

Back in the living room, Charlie picked the book up off the floor, and admitted to himself that it wasn't simply the warm comfort of the dog which had lulled him to sleep. He had never been much of a Bible reader, in large part because wading through the language was a real ordeal for him. This, being a pocket-sized edition with tiny print in two columns on each page, made it even harder to read.

On top of that, he had no idea what, if anything, he was looking for.

He started the examination all over again, first inspecting the covers, which were scuffed from use and greasy to the touch. Then he opened it and, for the first time, noticed that the first two pages were stuck together. Carefully peeling them apart, Charlie read, *The Holy Bible, New International Version*.

At the bottom of the page he saw something handwritten in pencil. The letters were very faint, but holding it directly under the light he was able to make out the words: *Prop. of Jas. Thos. MacLendon.*

Which had to be short for *James Thomas MacLendon*.

Jimmy Doe.

Charlie's pulse quickened as he carefully turned the page. The next one was filled with printed copyright information. *Wonder what kind of royalty checks God gets*, he thought. He could find no additional writing.

The page following that was the table of contents listing all the books of the New and Old Testaments in order of appearance.

On that page, at the bottom, was another written notation: *Prv 2813*. 2813 couldn't be a year, unless Jimmy MacLendon was a time traveler. And what did *Prv* signify?

Charlie's mind suddenly got a flash from the past, back to when he was a boy dutifully attending Sunday School with his mama and sister, and being generally bored with the entire proposition, but knowing he daren't protest. God might not have boxed his ears, but Mama surely would've, had he complained. *John 3:16* was what he remembered. He didn't remember the entire passage, though the *For God so loved the world that he gave his only begotten son* part had been drummed into him. It was the *3:16* part that seemed significant now.

Chapter and verse.

Looking at the handwritten note, he imagined a colon between the *28* and the *13*. But that still left *Prv*. What did that signify?

Maybe Charlie should have paid more attention in Sunday School.

Then he saw it. The answer was right there on the page in front of him.

Proverbs.

Charlie flipped through the Bible until he came upon the Book of Proverbs, then thumbed his way to Chapter 28, and traced the words down with his finger until he saw '13' printed in bold numbers.

Whoever conceals his transgressions will not prosper, he read, *but he who confesses and forsakes them will obtain mercy*.

That seemed like a fairly generic kind of Biblical passage — confess your sins and you'll be forgiven — but it must have meant something more to Jimmy.

Then Charlie noticed the faint marks on the page.

Certain passages had been underlined

in pencil. Working back and forth from the thirteenth verse, he saw that the underlines went all through Chapter 28, but did not extend to the next one. Neither were any visible in Chapter 27. At first glance the words appeared to be selected at random, but he suspected that was not the case. Rushing to the small desk that was tucked into the corner of his dining area, Charlie found a pencil of his own and a pad of paper, and went to work.

★　★　★

Ramona Rios was on the floor covered in flowers.

She didn't even remember throwing herself to the side just as the muzzled shot was fired at her. She remembered with dreamlike imagery the sight of Michael Fleer appearing out of nowhere and chopping the hand of the shooter with his own, causing him to drop the gun. She also remembered Fleer grabbing the shooter in a headlock and spinning him around, which is why all the flowers were scattered on top of her. Ramona did not so much remember as hear the vicious punch to Michael's stomach which caused him to stagger, but she saw him recover enough to smash his fist upwards into the shooter's chin, which nearly caused the man to topple over backwards.

He remained upright, barely, though turned toward the door to catch himself. Then he simultaneously rose up and spun back around, both of his fists welded together to make a flesh-and-bone hammer, which he slammed into the side of Michael's head causing him to go down.

Ramona screamed his name as the would-be shooter lunged for his gun and pointed it once more at Ramona.

She had never seen this man before . . . why did he want to kill her?

Michael Fleer was moaning on the floor. Knowing these were her last seconds on Earth, and that there was no escape, she shut her eyes and waited for the end.

But then she heard the drunken voice of Ralph Scranton hollering, 'Now what the hell's going on?'

She opened her eyes again, and saw the

shooter look back and forth between her, the manager, and the FBI agent who had pulled himself to his knees. Instead of firing at everyone, the assailant turned, burst through the lobby door, and fled.

'You again!' Scranton cried upon seeing Ramona. 'Jesus, lady!'

'Someone just tried to kill me!' Ramona shouted back. 'He could have killed you, too!'

'What the hell are all these flowers doing on the floor?' the manager asked.

Michael Fleer, meanwhile, was on his knees, holding his head in his hands.

'Michael, are you alright?' she asked. 'Do you want me to call an ambulance?'

'No . . . I think I'm okay . . . but he knocked out my contacts . . . I can't see . . . without them.'

Ramona crouched down and helped him look, finding one soft lens on the floor. It looked like it had a spot of dirt on it. By the time she handed it to him, Fleer had found the other. He rose, staggered to a bench in the lobby, and from his pocket withdrew a lens holder. Taking a bottle of solution from another pocket, he squirted some into the holder and then dropped his lenses in, closing and shaking it. Procedure complete, he replaced them in his eyes.

'Oh, god,' he muttered, tearing up a bit. 'If the bureau knew I needed so much help seeing, they'd reassign me to a desk.'

'I won't tell anyone,' Ramona said. 'I think you saved my life.'

'Will somebody tell me what the hell this is all about?' Scranton shouted again. 'Rios, you're about a half inch away from being kicked out of here.'

Fleer rose shakily and flashed his badge at the man. 'It's above your level of understanding, sir,' he said.

'Ohhhhhh,' the manager moaned. 'Just what I need. Am I under arrest?'

"No. Why would you be?

'I don't know. I don't know anything. Maybe if I get drunk enough, James Bond'll show up.' With that Ralph Scranton turned and shuffled back to his unit.

'Are you sure you're all right, Michael?' Ramona asked.

'You know that old cliché about seeing

stars? Well, I had the entire galaxy for a while. But it's going away.'

'Did you see the person?'

'Yes, but I didn't recognize him. Since he was wearing gloves, there aren't going to be any prints anywhere.'

'The guy was a pro?'

'Not much of one,' the agent said. 'He had you in point blank range and didn't fire.'

'Maybe he didn't have enough bullets for all three of us.'

'Maybe,' Fleer said. 'Let's go back upstairs. I may need to lie down for a bit.'

'Sure,' she said, 'but let me get these first. I think I'm owed them.' Ramona quickly gathered up the flowers, orange gladioli, from the floor. Then she led Fleer to the elevator and punched the 'up' button.

Back in her apartment, she dropped the flowers on the counter and turned to the agent. 'Okay, not that I'm complaining, but how did you magically appear in the lobby?'

'I didn't think you should go down there on your own, so I followed,' he said, stretching out on her sofa. 'You were already in the elevator, so I found the stairs. I was behind you when I saw him pull the gun, so I sprang into action. I pushed you out of the line of fire and spun around so I didn't get shot in your place, and then disarmed him.'

'You pushed me down?'

'Would you rather have been shot? The irony is that I could have shot and wounded him first but I gave you my gun. I'm so used to wearing it at all times, I didn't even remember I was no longer carrying it.'

'Oh, yeah. It's in my purse,' she said.

Fleer went over to her bag and retrieved his weapon, sliding it back in its holster.

'The real irony,' Ramona countered, 'is that the damn police were just here, literally minutes before the guy showed up.'

'It's almost as though he was outside, watching, and waiting for them to leave, isn't it?' Fleer said, with a slight tone of raspy sarcasm.

'All right, all right, don't rub it in. What

made you so convinced I was in danger in the first place?'

'Ramona, the flower delivery gambit is the oldest pretense there is. I've used it myself a time or two, while looking for someone. You claimed someone fired at you in the parking garage, and then that same day flowers come to the door. I decided it was better to be safe than to have you in a body bag, even if I ran off unarmed.'

'The police didn't believe the first attempt, but now that I have a witness, they'll believe this one!' she said, going for her telephone.

Fleer stopped her. 'No, I'm sorry, but I don't think you should call them.'

'Why not? This was a genuine attempt on my life!'

'I know, but like you said, they didn't believe you the first time. So leave the police out of this and let me handle it. I know a little about what you're up against.'

Marching over to her chair, Ramona plopped down, crossed her legs, and said, 'All right, I've had enough teasing. *What*

214

is going on? What have I stumbled upon that's worth someone killing me?'

Fleer paced back and forth for a moment, then said, 'The bureau has been investigating some high-level improprieties in the city of Los Angeles for the better part of two years now, and everything seems to lead to one man.'

'Let me guess . . . Nick Cantone, right?'

Fleer shook his head. 'I'm talking about Alberto Soto.'

'The mayor of Los Angeles?'

'The soon-to-be ex-mayor of Los Angeles,' Michael Fleer said.

*　*　*

When Charlie Grosvenor had finished writing down all the passages of the twenty-eighth chapter of Proverbs that had been deliberately underlined, he read it back:

> The wicked flee through . . . a
> driving rain . . . evildoers do not
> understand what is right . . . the
> rich whose ways are perverse . . .

*will fall into their own trap . . . the
rich . . . how deluded they are
. . . anyone tormented by guilt . . .
is partner to one who destroys
. . . those who trust in themselves
are fools . . . but those who close
their eyes to them receive many
curses.*

While the underlined segments made
an eerie sort of sense, there was no
determining exactly what they were
meant to convey. Still, several complete
thoughts appeared to be represented.
Charlie wrote the words out again, only
this time adding some punctuation in
places that seemed to call for it. What he
got was:

*The wicked flee through a driving
rain. Evildoers do not understand
what is right. The rich, whose ways
are perverse, will fall into their own
trap. The rich . . . how deluded
they are! Anyone tormented by guilt
is partner to one who destroys.
Those who trust in themselves are*

*fools, but those who close their eyes
to them receive many curses.*

This time Charlie was struck by the
specifics. Why did the wicked flee through
'a driving rain?' Why was that detail important? Similarly, why was there repetition
of the word *rich?*

After looking at the message, if that was
really what it was, Charlie had another
idea. Tearing off the page on which he
had written the passage, he read it out
loud while writing down a more modern
interpretation of the words, almost like a
translation. He tried not to think hard
about it, simply writing down the first
thing that came to his mind. When he was
done, he read it back, and then, on a
whim, erased certain words and replaced
them with others, in order to change the
text to past tense.

*Evil people fled through a rain-
storm not knowing right from
wrong. The rich are always bad and
someday they will get caught, even
if they're deluded about it. One*

who feels guilty was along with
another one who destroyed some-
thing. Trusting yourself is foolish,
but turning a blind eye means
you're damned.

Could that be meant as a reference to Jimmy's bad eye?

Charlie doubted it. There was a passage somewhere in the bible about plucking out your own eye if it offends you, wasn't there? If Jimmy was looking to use scripture to describe himself, it seemed like that would be a better fit.

Looking at it again, this time Charlie's attention was grabbed by the word *partner*. Every other reference to two different kinds of people was in the plural, which made sense, since the Scriptures were all about defining those who are unrepentant sinners and those who were saved. But *partner* was singular, as was *one who destroys*.

Suddenly the difference between *wicked* and *evildoers* seemed significant as well.

What if the message was not meant to indicate two groups of people, but rather two individuals, one of whom might be as guilty as his partner of something, but not necessarily because he was evil?

Looking at it from this perspective, Charlie wrote down another interpretation, this time in his own words.

Upon reading it back, he felt chilled.

> *Two people who did something bad were driving through the rain to run away from it. One of them is evil with no concept of right and wrong. The evil one is also rich, so he thinks he can get away with it, but someday he will trap himself. The friend of the criminal has a conscience, but his partner foolishly assumed his wealth would allow him to escape judgment. The friend said nothing about the crime to anyone (maybe 'closing his eyes' for money), and suffers as a result.*

One partner was evil and committed a horrible crime, that the merely wicked partner covered up. It seemed obvious that Jimmy was the wicked, but not evil one, since he was the one worried about forgiveness. The one with a conscience.

But who was the other? And what had they done?

Maybe Jimmy had left more messages in the form of underlined words somewhere else in the little book.

Charlie certainly didn't feel like going though page by page, so he turned back to the contents page so see if he had missed any other shorthand notations.

No others were visible.

Then something struck his eye. It could only be seen when he held the book a certain way. It was a smudge, maybe a finger mark, over the word *Revelation* on the contents page.

Revelation, the last book of the Bible, and as best Charlie could remember, the one that described all hell breaking loose.

His upper lip perspiring, Charlie Grosvenor thumbed to it and carefully turned the pages until he again came upon two that were stuck together. Carefully pulling them apart, he saw something tucked in between them. It was a yellowed piece of newsprint.

Dislodging it, he saw that it was a

newspaper clipping, quite old and very brittle. A tear on the bottom had been repaired with tape. Holding it as carefully as possible, Charlie began to read, his head unconsciously shaking back and forth as he did so.

'Lord have mercy,' he whispered when he was done.

★ ★ ★

Gunnar Fesche's jaw hurt like hell, and his lower teeth ached. He hoped the guy who had given him the pile-driver upper-cut had broken his goddamned hand in the process.

Still, he was not sorry he didn't finish the job then and there. The hit had to be done the right way, and dropping a mark in front of *two* witnesses, both of whom could see his face, was not the right way.

But what was it with this damn woman?

She was like a cat with nine lives.

Or could it be *him*?

Christ, was he subconsciously screwing up because he'd never before had to take out a woman?

Fesche rejected that idea. A job was a job. Period.

Sitting in his car, across the street from the soon-to-be-dead woman's apartment, he wished he had an ice pack for his chin. Even wrapping the ice from a fast-food restaurant coke in a handkerchief would help. Maybe he should just go the hell back to his hotel, soak his face in a sink full of ice, and come back another day. Cantone might not be happy, but Cantone's jaw didn't feel like it had been hit with a tire iron.

So focused was Gunnar Fesche on his own problem that he almost missed the Rios woman and her Feddy friend leaving the apartment building.

The bastard hardly looked the worse for wear.

They went down to a black Audi parked on the street and got in, the guy behind the wheel. As the car pulled away from the curb, Fesche started his own vehicle up and followed them. Wherever they were going, he'd be right behind.

14

Ramona Rios showed up at the building owned by Charlie Grosvenor a little after six.

Fleer had driven her, though he opted not to go on and meet the man. He said it was safer that way.

When Charlie answered the door, he did a double take.

'What now?' he asked.

'Charlie, I need a place to bunk.'

'You're kidding.'

'It's not safe staying at my apartment.'

She filled him in on what had transpired that day, and he said, 'Damn, girl, get in here.'

Once they were inside, she said, 'I can sleep on the couch. It's no problem.'

'No, I've had somebody just move out, so there's an empty unit upstairs,' he told her. 'It's not the Ritz, but it gets the job done.'

'What do you mean *you* have an empty

unit? You make it sound like you own this
. . . oh, my god, you *do*, don't you?'

'I own this place, and a few others
around downtown,' he said, 'and I don't
do it to make money. I lose money, and it
don't matter. I'm independently wealthy.
Someday I'll tell you why, along with my
full name, but Charlie still sticks. Now, do
you want the unit or not?'

'Uh, yes, please.'

'Fine. You can stay there as long as you
want. I see you don't have any kind of a
bag, though.'

She held up her purse. 'This is it for
now. I can sneak back and get things
later.'

*Or just live like us, wearing the same
clothes until they have to be surgically sepa-
rated from our bodies*, Charlie thought,
but he said nothing.

Pooch came up to her, looking
apprehensive, but slowly wagging his tail.
'Who's this, Charlie?'

'That's Pooch. He's just moved in, too.
Don't ask me how or why, I just live here.'

Ramona held her hand out to Pooch,
who sniffed it, and then rolled over on his

back. She rubbed his belly and his tail began to conduct Sousa.

'What a sweet dog!' she said.

'Yeah,' Charlie said, 'he's just one of today's surprises.'

'What else happened?'

'I know who Jimmy was. And I know his secret.'

'How'd you find out?'

'Read it in the Good Book.'

She shook her head. 'Okay. Mind if I use your bathroom before you start preaching?'

Charlie smiled. 'I ain't gonna preach. The jakes's through that door, there.'

When Ramona returned, Charlie asked her to sit down in the living room. He then told her the story of obtaining Jimmy MacLendon's Bible . . . and Pooch . . . and how he found an underlined message in Proverbs. Then he handed her the newspaper clipping.

Deadly hit-and-run on Sunset the headline read.

Los Angeles — The body of a twenty-three-year-old woman was found dead early this morning on the Rustic Canyon area of Sunset Boulevard, the apparent victim of a hit-and-run accident. Police say injuries suffered by Deborah Questal, a *UCLA* student, were commensurate with her having been struck and run over by a vehicle moving at a high rate of speed.

Yesterday's unexpected rainstorm is thought to have been a factor in the accident, which is believed to have happened between one and two a.m., according to Sgt. Steve Turcott of the LAPD's Western division. 'We are encouraging anyone who might have seen, or even heard something pertaining to this tragedy to contact the police or the county sheriff's department,' Turcott said.

'You think Jimmy knew something about this hit-and-run?' Ramona asked.

'I think poor old Jim was in the car that hit her,' Charlie said. 'I think he was with somebody and they hit the woman and then fled the scene, and Jimmy was forced to keep his mouth shut about it, or maybe paid to keep his mouth shut. I think the guilt haunted him for years. And here's why I think that.' He handed the papers on which he'd translated the message to Ramona. 'See if you agree with that conclusion.'

'My god, this is creepy,' she said, setting the pages down. 'This other person in the car, the rich guy, I don't suppose Jimmy spelled his name out, or anything, did he?'

'I don't think identifying him was Jimmy's aim. I don't think he expected anyone else to find this. I think this was a personal message to himself, maybe to read or recite over again, like all that stuff the Catholics make you say to wash the sin blackboard clean.'

'Father Carreras never puts it quite that way.'

'Oh, sorry if I offended you.'

She shrugged. 'It's a pretty good metaphor, actually.'

She picked up the newspaper clipping again and turned it over.

'Governor, did you look at the back?' she asked.

'No. Why?'

'The date of the newspaper is here. It's been folded over.' With a fingernail, she carefully lifted a paper panhandle from the top of clipping and straightened it. 'June 30, 1975. Thirty years ago. Could this be the reason Jimmy was killed? Because he knew about this?'

'That's the sixty-four-thousand dollar question. You're probably too young to even know what that means.'

'It was an old TV game show, wasn't it?'

Charlie looked impressed. 'Yeah. I thought you had to be my age to know that.'

'I took a broadcast history class in college.'

'You know, I've been worrying so much about my discovery I haven't been a very good host. I don't get a lot of practice. Do you want something to drink? I have soda, milk, or I can make coffee.'

'Water's fine.'

Charlie got a bottle from the fridge and handed it to her.

'Now, then,' he said, 'since we're

talking about murders, what's all this about someone shooting at you?'

'It seems I'm on the mayor's hit list,' she said.

'The mayor? Of Los Angeles? Richard Riordan wants you dead?'

'No, Charlie, Riordan's been gone four years. The current mayor is Alberto Soto. I guess you don't vote.'

'I don't. But the mayor putting a contract out on somebody, damn, that's pretty extreme.'

She took a sip of water and affected an expression that indicated deep thought. Then she said, 'I know. The FBI agent who saved my life . . . he's the one who brought me here, by the way, and he's probably outside somewhere, waiting for me to come out . . . anyway, he said the bureau has been investigating Soto for quite a while because of alleged ties to a Mexican drug cartel. He seems to think that Phoenix Terrace, that downtown development that Nick Cantone is developing, is being built on a piece of property that Soto was eyeing to put up his own hotel, which would be a money-laundering venue for the Mexican mob. Michael . . . that's the agent's name, Michael Fleer . . . said that my reporting on the project meant I was getting close to the truth, so I had to be eliminated.'

'Hmm. Ramona, if you don't mind my saying so, this sounds a little bit like the plot of a movie, and not a particularly good one.'

'I know. When Michael told me all this, I believed it, because, well, the guy had just saved my life. But the more I think about it, the less it holds up. My reporting has been critical of the Phoenix project and Cantone, particularly the rumor that homeless people were being bused out of Skid Row and dumped before the television cameras show up. That friend of ours, Danny Speakman, told me that part was true because, when he was in his Aspen disguise, he got bused somewhere too. But that's why it doesn't make sense.'

'You've lost me.'

'If my reporting shines a bad enough light on Cantone and Phoenix Terrace to put the project in jeopardy, then shouldn't that benefit Soto . . . who can then put his plan to build on the site into action? Why would he be the one who wants to have me killed?'

'Maybe you uncovered something you don't realize you uncovered.'

'I can't imagine what. I mean, if anybody wanted me out of the way, it would be Adam Henry, the state assemblyman who's running for mayor. You know, the former action movie star who retired when his age started to get higher than his IQ?'

Charlie chuckled. 'I've seen him in things. What did you do to him?'

'Revealed that he is so dumb he thinks Manual Labor is the president of Mexico. Or at least allowed him to reveal it on camera.'

'One doesn't have to be a genius to get elected.'

'I know, but here's an example of just how bright the guy is. I've done some research on him. Adam Henry isn't his real name. He took it when he started acting. His real name is Henry Baron Bonesteel.'

'What's so dumb about changing your name?'

'Nothing, but he could have been Henry Baron, or Hank Steele, or Barry Steele, or something that wasn't an L.A. sheriff's department code word.'

'I'm not following.'

''Adam Henry' is county slang for 'asshole,'' Ramona said. 'It's what sheriffs say to each other over the radio, and Adam Henry doesn't even know it!'

That drew an actual laugh from Charlie Grosvenor, which was a rare occurrence.

'How many people over the years have been laughing behind his back, but haven't said anything, because he's a big, rich movie star?'

Suddenly Charlie Grosvenor stopped laughing. 'You didn't tell the police you'd be staying here with me, did you?'

'No. I made the decision to come here kind of spur of the moment. I haven't told anyone. Why?'

'They know me as a streeter. Police reports are public record. I don't want someone to find out who I really am and write it up in a report and then have it leak out.'

'You're not D. B. Cooper, are you?'

'Who?'

'Never mind. The police don't know where I am because I didn't call them after the last murder attempt, so you're safe.'

'You didn't file a report?'

'Michael said not to. He said he would handle things.'

'That's strange.'

'I reported the first two shots taken at me and the police came out to investigate. They found no evidence of any kind, so they have me pegged as an hysterical woman. Maybe even crazy, given the trick I played on the sketch artist. Because of that, I doubt they'd believe anything else I said.'

'Even with the agent backing you up?'

'He doesn't seem to like the police much,' she said. 'At least he doesn't want to work with them. I guess it's one of those local versus fed things. Or maybe he thinks the LAPD is somehow involved in whatever conspiracy is going on.'

Charlie Grosvenor was frowning. 'I have to tell you, Ramona, something here's not right. I'm no expert on this stuff but this guy of yours sounds like he's acting more as a rogue than an agent. How'd you meet him again?'

'He was just there, outside my apartment when the police were investigating.'

'Did he show you a badge?'

'Yes.'

'You study it?'

'I saw it. I didn't study it. What are you thinking?'

'He drove you here, dropped you off, but didn't want to come inside and introduce himself. Didn't want to see me.'

'He doesn't know you.'

'What if he does, and that's why? What's this guy look like?'

'He looks like the actor from *Angel*,' Ramona said. 'Tall, well-built, dark hair cut short, military style, not a lot of expression.'

'What about his eyes?'

'Brown.'

'You sure?'

'Yes, I saw them. Oh, and he wears contact lenses, too. He said he's nearly blind without them. What's bothering you, Charlie?'

'The fact that there's a guy who just shows up all of a sudden like and then disappears with no warning again. Sounds like someone I know.'

'Well, Danny did that to me, but — '

She stopped talking and looked at the governor.

'You see it now, too,' he said.

'Oh, my god! His contacts . . . they were knocked out during the fight with my assailant and he had to find them. I knew he looked familiar, but I decided it was a resemblance to that actor, David someone. But that's not why he looked familiar. And those contacts weren't because he's myopic, they were — '

'To change his blue eyes brown,' Charlie finished for her.

'Oh, Jesus! I picked up one of the contacts and thought it was dirty, but that wasn't dirt, it was brown coloration! He shaved his beard off, he buzzed his hair and dyed it black, he put in contacts, and I fell for it!'

'You didn't recognize his voice?'

Ramona put her head in her hands. 'Raspy, almost like he had laryngitis. He

235

disguised that, too. God, what an idiot I've been! It was Danny all along! Charlie, we have to go talk to Detective Knight no matter what anyone else thinks about it.'

'I think you're right about that,' he replied. 'I'll go call for a ride to the station. We could walk it if we wanted but my little voice is telling me we shouldn't.'

★ ★ ★

Sitting in his car, which was pulled up outside of the governor's apartment building, the man listened to the conversation going on inside through an earpiece. He wanted to find out exactly what the Rios woman knew, or thought she knew.

He found out.

One part of him was glad those two had figured it out so quickly. He knew Ramona was going to find the bug he'd dropped in her purse eventually, probably sooner rather than later. But the other part of him, the part that had been assigned to take care of problems, was reeling at how much they had accurately deduced. An old bastard who apparently only pretended to be a bagman and a TV reporter barely old enough to have covered Bush v. Gore had somehow pieced things together.

To a point.

A point beyond which he could not allow them to go.

As he heard the governor calling on the phone for a cab to take them to the police station, he still wondered just what this guy's story really was. But he could not waste a lot of time wondering.

Nor could he waste time chastising himself for not taking the Bible that his stinking, walleyed prey tried to defend himself with, when he stabbed him in his box. There's no way he could have known what it contained.

But once he had taken care of them, he'd find the damn little book and destroy it.

And there was certainly no purpose in telling his employer about it before he did.

15

Seated in the back of the taxi, Ramona Rios cut off the call on her cell phone and said, 'Knight isn't there right now. He gets off at six-thirty, but they're going to find him.'

Charlie Grosvenor, who was next to her with Jimmy's Bible in his hands, simply nodded his head.

When she dropped her phone back into her purse, they both heard the odd *clink* made by the phone striking something hard. Investigating, Ramona came upon the tiny microphone device and pulled it out.

'I don't believe this,' she said. 'This is a damn bug!'

She started to roll down the window to throw it out, but Charlie stopped her.

'No, no, hang onto it,' he advised. 'More evidence for the cops.'

'Is the prick still listening?'

'If he is, he knows where we're going. I

don't think he'd pull anything in a police station.'

'I hope he is listening!' she said, suddenly angry. Holding the bug to her mouth, Ramona unleashed a string of expletives, a few of which Charlie had never before heard.

'Damn,' he uttered, half-admiringly.

They were still a couple blocks away from the Central Community Station. Neither was paying much attention when suddenly the taxi slammed to a halt, and the driver laid on the horn.

'What's going on?' Ramona asked.

'Someone just zoomed around me and cut me off!' the driver called back. Rolling down the window, he shouted, *Idiot!*'

The other driver, whose Audi was stopped perpendicular to the taxi's nose, leapt out from behind the wheel.

'Oh, my god!' Ramona shouted, but there was nothing she could do to get away from the other driver who was charging the taxi with a gun.

'Jesus!' the driver yelled as the man who called himself Michael Fleer, among other things, slammed the barrel of the gun into the driver's window, causing it to shatter.

'The two of you get out of the back or the front seat gets a brain shower,' Fleer snarled, holding the gun against the driver's temple.

'Don't shoot,' the driver burbled. 'I have a family.'

'Rios, Governor, I said get out. Now.'

He cocked the gun.

'All right,' Ramona said, opening the door and stepping out onto the street. 'It's not dark yet. Someone's going to see what you're doing!'

'A smart guy once told me nobody sees anything on Skid Row, and even if they do, they keep it to themselves. Isn't that right, Governor?'

'I wish you hadn't been listening, Aspen,' Charlie said, surreptitiously tucking the bible into the waist of his pants behind him as he slid over and climbed out.

When they were on the street, the driver asked, 'Can I go now?'

'Sure,' Fleer replied. 'Here's your send-off.'

He shot the man through the head.

Ramona screamed and Fleer spun around and pointed the gun at her.

'You damn punk!' Charlie spat.

'Now you know I'm serious,' Fleer said. 'Get in the backseat of my car, Rios. Now. You don't make a move, old man.'

Ramona's legs barely carried her to the Audi.

Turning to Charlie, the one-time Aspen said, 'Can you drive, Pops?'

'I haven't for a long time.'

'Do your best. Get behind the wheel.' He pointed to the Audi.

'You didn't have to shoot him, Aspen.'

'That same smart guy once told me what life is worth on Skid Row, too. I'll put one through this bitch's head if you don't do what I tell you,' Fleer said.

'Look, son, let's just take a breath and — '

'I'll shoot her, goddammit! I've got you pegged, Pops. You're the noble type who would sacrifice himself if that's what it took to save others. That's why I'm not giving you the opportunity. So you'll either do what I say or she's the one who will be sacrificed, you get it?'

'Charlie, don't worry about me,' Ramona said.

'Too late, baby girl,' Charlie sighed, getting behind the wheel of the Audi. Fleer forced Ramona into the back at gunpoint, then joined her.

'We're going back to her apartment,' Fleer said.

'Why there?' Ramona asked.

'Because I said so. Pops, I'll feed you the directions, and if you make one wrong turn or try to do anything heroic, Chi-Chi gets a bullet in the *cabeza*.'

The keys were still in the ignition, so Charlie Grosvenor turned it over and lurched the Audi ahead. It had to be thirty years minimum since he had driven a car, but that wasn't the thing that was eating him up inside. Concern of what would happen to Ramona was causing his chest to tighten, as was the growing sense of guilt that he had lured the taxi driver to his death.

As he battled with the Audi's hair-trigger brakes and a steering wheel so sensitive it could be controlled telepathically, Charlie

Grosvenor wondered if he was going to see the sunrise.

*   *   *

'I'm assuming you called me up here to give me a thumbs down on that press conference,' Adam Henry was saying as he stretched his legs out in front of the sienna, full-grain leather sofa in Nick Cantone's private office in the Harrison Club. If he was apprehensive about this meeting, he did not show it.

'You almost sound as though you wish I would,' Cantone said.

'God's honest truth, Nicky? I wish we could drop this entire thing. I don't want to be mayor. I never wanted to be mayor. I wouldn't know how. Why can't I simply drop out of the race to spend more time with my family?'

'Which one?'

Henry grimaced as he took a sip of his bourbon. 'I broke it off with Consuela,' he said. 'She's promised to take the boy somewhere far away. That damn kid is getting to look more like me every day. Even

Marsha was starting to notice anytime he came over while his mother was cleaning the house.' Marsha Creighton was Henry's wife, and the mother of his three legitimate children. 'But you didn't ask me up here to talk about my love child.'

'Nor did I to hear any talk of your quitting,' Cantone said. 'Listen to me, Adam. I believe your instincts are right. You wouldn't know how to be mayor. With a manual at your disposal, you wouldn't know. But you don't have to be a good mayor. All you have to do is what I tell you to do. The problem is that in order to be mayor, you have to be a mayoral candidate. And you, my friend, are proving to be an even worse candidate than you are an actor.'

'Hey, you hold on a minute. I got a Golden Globe for — '

'You can't even act the role of a candidate!' Cantone shouted, and once he had reduced Adam Henry to cowering silence, he quieted down himself. 'That is going to change, Adam. That's why I called you up here. You are going to start an intensive course in candidate training.'

'A what?'

'I've engaged political and media consultants to coach you. By the time they're through, you will be able to send Slick Willie home licking his wounds after a debate, let alone that sob-sister Al Soto.'

'Is that really necessary?' Henry asked.

Nick Cantone slammed his fist down on a Chippendale table, nearly shattering it, causing Henry to jump.

'I need a mayor whose ass I can stick my hand up to make him talk like Kermit the Frog,' Cantone growled. 'That is not simply something I *want*. It is something I *need*. It is something I *will* get. Phoenix Terrace is only the beginning of this city's transformation in my image. But I cannot fulfill my plans without someone at the top looking out for my interests, and that is why *you* are going to be L.A.'s next mayor, Adam, whether you like it or not. I have invested far too much into this, and into you, to have anything go wrong now. Alberto Soto must be thrown out of office if I am to get anything done before I'm too damned old to enjoy the results and you are the only person who can do it.

The camera loves you even when you dare it not to. Therefore, I am not asking you to take candidate classes, Adam. I am telling you.'

Henry drained his glass and set it down on the coffee table. 'Purely hypothermally — '

'Hypo*thetically*, for Christ's sake!'

'Okay, but what would happen if I said no?'

Nick Cantone leveled his very practiced gaze on the former actor. It was the same look he used in boardroom meetings when somebody demonstrated the sheer stupidity of disagreeing with him. The goal was to remain silent and hold the gaze until the other person squirmed. His record was three minutes and forty-two seconds, after which the recalcitrant board member (ex-board member by week's end) actually leapt up as though the chair had suddenly become molten through x-ray vision.

It took only twenty-nine seconds for Adam Henry to flinch.

Cantone smiled thinly. 'In the unthinkable event that you refuse me, Adam, I will destroy you entirely. Surely you can see it from my perspective. If you genuinely become of no use to me, then I have nothing to lose by running you through the shredder. All I have to do is leak a little bit of information that I've been able to discover about some past problems of yours, and leave you to defend yourself against the D.A.'s office.'

'Past . . . you can't know that.'

'I can't know what?'

'You can't know about that night . . . in the rain . . . after the party. There's no way you could know. Only two people knew about that, and one's dead. I saw to that myself!'

It was a very rare occurrence that Nick Cantone was taken by surprise, but he had to admit this was one of those very unusual moments. He decided to bluff. 'You'd be surprised and, ideally, terrified at what I can find out. But perhaps you should confirm whether my information is correct. We are both talking about that night of the wild party . . . '

Henry's lip was shiny with perspiration. 'In 1975, yeah, the party in the Palisades, where I really tied one on, and Mac MacLendon told me I shouldn't drive home, but I got behind the wheel anyway. It was raining, the road was wet, and on Sunset Boulevard there was this girl by the side of the road trying to flag us down. Mac was yelling at me, 'Bone, slow down!' Back then we played a few clubs as Mac and Bone.'

'Bone . . . of course,' Cantone improvised.

'That was my name, Bonesteel. Friends called me Bone. But you knew that.'

'Of course I did,' Cantone smoothly lied.

The former Henry Baron Bonesteel wiped his lip with this sleeve, and then continued.

'I just wanted to scare the woman, but . . . '

'You hit her,' Cantone said, guessing, but doing so with authority. 'You hit her and killed her.'

'Christ, Nick, how did you find that out? Did you talk to Mac? Jesus, did I kill him so he didn't talk *too late*? You have no idea what I thought when I saw him down on Skid Row. At first I didn't know who he was cause I'd heard he was dead. All those years I thought I was safe, especially after I changed my name. Then a few weeks ago, I was down there on the site of the Phoenix thing, posing for some pictures — '

'What are you talking about?' Cantone snapped. 'I didn't authorize any photo shoot.'

'I know . . . it was my own idea,' Henry said. 'I thought if I could get some photos looking around at the blight in Skid Row, I could release them during the campaign to prove that I'm someone who's going to take on the big issues as mayor.'

'Oh, good god.'

'No, it's a good thing, Nick, because that's when I saw the walleyed little creep. He was a bum, a Skid Row bum. He came walking up to me and I didn't even recognize him at first, 'cause like I said, I thought he was dead. But he knew me, which I didn't think much about, because I'm a movie star. I get recognized all the time. But he said, 'Bone, it's me! It's Mac!' Then I noticed his eye. Mac always had a crooked eye, even when he was young, but now it pointed straight to the side. It was him, all right. I thought I was going to fall down. He said, 'Look what's happened to me, Bone. It's my punishment from God. How did you escape it?' I said something like, 'You're mistaken,' and turned and ran. But it was him. So tell me, Nicky. You got your information from him, right? There's no other way.'

Cantone drew in a long, slow breath, and let it out even more slowly.

'There was one other way, Adam,' he said. 'I got it from you, just now.'

'You . . . didn't know about the hit-and-run?'

'Not until one minute ago.'

'Oh, for . . . '

'What my team dug up on you was that you were the primary drug supplier for Leslie Malk and Associates Casting while you were in college at UC San Diego, bringing the stuff up from Mexico for Leslie to distribute throughout Hollywood. This made you so wealthy you didn't need to bother finishing college. After you dealt your way into an acting career, I also learned about that time you were coked to high heaven and roughed up a prostitute while on location in Old Tuscon for a film. You roughed her up enough to cause her to miscarry.'

'Christ. I paid her off, too.'

Cantone nodded. 'Forty-five thousand dollars. But I digress. Let's go back to your friend Mac for a moment. Tell me exactly what you mean when you said 'I killed him not to talk.''

'I didn't do it personally,' Henry said, wiping his lip again. 'I hired it out. Found a guy who posed as a Skid Row bum long enough to find Mac and take care of him, and he did.'

'Is this hit man of yours by any chance about sixty and black?'

'What? No, he's a young guy. Good looking, blond. Could have been an actor himself.'

'Why didn't you tell me all this up front?' Cantone asked.

'I thought you might be disappointed if you knew.'

'So you took it all upon yourself to hire a hit man to take care of your secret, a

251

secret even I didn't know.'

'That show's initiative, doesn't it?'

'What's his name, Adam?'

'Well, I don't know if he wants me spreading his name around.'

Nick Cantone turned on the high-beam glare again, and after a half-minute, Henry said, 'Alex Tunzi, but he has a lot of other names he uses. Why do you want to know his name?'

So I can be sure it is not the same man I hired to kill Ramona Rios, you side of rotting beef, Cantone thought, but said nothing. Massaging his forehead, Cantone silently wished he could ask Fesche to take out Adam Henry, too, before he wrecked absolutely everything. But he could not. He simply had too much invested in this moron, and there was too much at stake ahead.

But *oh*, how he wished Steven Seagal had returned his call . . .

★　★　★

Charlie Grosvenor had carefully followed every one of the gunman's directions,

252

though he took care not to drive fast, which meant that it was nearly eight by the time they arrived at Ramona's apartment building.

'How do you open the garage door?' asked Alex Tunzi, alias Aspen, Danny Speakman, Ken Corder, and Michael Fleer. He still had the gun pointed at her.

'A key card,' Ramona replied. 'It's in my purse.'

'Get it. Slowly.'

Picking her purse up off the floor of the car, she reached in and found the card. Then on instruction, she handed it up to the governor who used it to open the garage door.

'Park in any open space,' Tunzi ordered. 'Even if it's handicapped. I won't be here that long.'

'Why are we here in the first place?' Ramona asked. 'Why not just kill us back on Skid Row?'

'Because that would draw too much attention. The cops and the press would be all over the discovery of two more bodies, and that might cause a delay in the development projects. Besides, you were already shot at down here once. This time it was successful.'

'Shot at by you?'

'No. Honestly, Chi-Chi, I don't know who the flower man is.'

'I guess I'll take your word for it,' Ramona said, trying to stall for time, 'but can I ask one more thing?'

'Please don't disappoint me by begging for your life.'

'I just want to know your real name. And whether this is your real hair, cut and dyed, or whether you were wearing a wig as Danny.'

'It won't hurt now. Alexander Tunzi. Pleased to meet you. And no, this isn't the real me. I had my hair butched and dyed. You figured out the part about my eyes.'

'You were listening to us,' Ramona said, as Charlie pulled into an empty slot.

'Yeah. I wanted to know exactly what you knew. I hung around you at that press conference for the same reason, until you started to wreck everything, and there was nothing I could do to get you to stop. Now get out, both of you.'

Ramona and Charlie exited the car, as did Tunzi, who kept his gun trained on Ramona.

'Mind if I ask a question now?' Charlie said, pronouncing *ask* as *axe*. 'You are the one who killed poor Jimmy, aren't you?'

'I was hired to.'

'By who?'

'By Nick Cantone,' Ramona said.

'Wrong, Chi-Chi,' Tunzi said. 'My employer is the next mayor.'

'You're *working* for Soto? So all that business about him and the Mexican cartels was just bull?'

'I don't know if it's bull or not. I don't know anything about Soto. Soto isn't my problem. Only his replacement, Adam Henry. He recognized the little bum as someone he used to know — who could dredge up an old scandal that would wreck his life. So the little bum had to go.'

'Sweet Jesus, that's it!' Charlie said. 'Adam Henry was the evildoer! He was the one driving the car Jimmy was riding in. He hit that poor young woman and killed her. And as long as Jim knew that a murderer was running for mayor, he couldn't be allowed to live.'

'In a nutshell,' Tunzi said. 'I found him and took him out, and then pretended to find his body as cover. Even you didn't really think I killed him, did you, Governor?'

'I didn't. Fact is, I told the police if you were the killer, you must be an Oscar winning actor. You had me fooled.'

'Yeah, well, I was able to rehearse.'

'Rehearse? How?'

'I practised first on a few other bums to make sure I knew exactly where to put the shiv, and where to stand so as not to get spattered by the blood.'

'You . . . killed other men . . . for *practice*?' Ramona said.

Tunzi smiled. 'Real serial killer, aren't I? Look, what's life even worth for a bum on the streets? I knew I had to get MacLendon right first time, so I couldn't take a chance on screwing it up.'

'How many?'

'Three, four, who cares? Okay, smarties, I know what you're doing, keeping me talking, but I can't screw up here, either. You two were never part of the plan, and truth is, I kind of liked both of you. Still, you know too much, so . . . ' he raised his gun.

But before he could fire, Alex Tunzi's head exploded.

Ramona screamed, and Gunnar Fesche walked out of the shadows of the parking garage, a tendril of smoke snaking up from the end of the silencer on his automatic pistol.

'Looks like I returned the favor, Ms. Rios,' he said.

'You're the flower man,' she said.

'And you're the dead woman.'

Fesche raised the gun.

She reached out and grabbed Charlie, then dived onto to the garage floor, pulling him with her as a bullet zoomed over their heads. 'He's a terrible shot,' she whispered. 'Roll under a car.'

'You roll, baby girl,' he said. 'I'm getting tired of this.'

Goddamned cat! Fesche thought, furiously.

Ramona wedged herself under the Audi, while Charlie crawled toward Tunzi's corpse and rolled it over. Another bullet missed his head by mere centimeters, but struck the body of the dead hitman. With the corpse on its back, Charlie was now able to take Tunzi's gun and return fire.

'Your odds just changed,' Charlie shouted, his voice echoing throughout the parking garage.

'You're not even part of this contract!' Fesche called back. 'Who the hell are you, anyway?'

'I'm the governor.'

'Yeah, and I'm the president.'

Charlie Grosvenor slowly stood up, keeping the automatic trained on his assailant. 'What's it gonna be, man?' he asked.

Fesche said nothing. He simply stood there, his gun pointed at Charlie's head, trying to figure out his best course of action. Noticing the slight tremor in the old, black man's hand as he held the gun — either from age or fear — he opted to take the risk.

Gunnar Fesche started to squeeze the trigger.

As he did, the garage door behind him

began to open, the sudden, unfamiliar noise startling him.

The shot went wild.

Charlie's didn't.

As the car pulled into the garage, its headlights backlit the sight of Gunnar Fesche sinking to the floor, howling in agony from the gunshot wound to his groin.

The driver of the car, a blonde woman, got out and shouted, 'What is this? Are you shooting a movie?'

'No ma'am,' Charlie called back, 'and we'd appreciate it if you'd go find the manager then call the police. And you might want to back on out and park on the street.'

By now, Ramona had crawled out from underneath the Audi.

'My clothes and I have spent entirely too much time this evening on the floor of this bunker,' she grumbled. Then she saw Fesche, who was rolling around in a fetal position, whimpering. 'Wow, Charlie, you sure know how to hurt a guy.'

'I was aiming for his knee,' Charlie said. 'I'm not much of a shot either.'

Then his legs weakened and he started to collapse, clutching his chest. Ramona caught him halfway down and eased him to the concrete floor.

16

Charlie Grosvenor was taken to the same hospital as Gunnar Fesche. What Ramona Rios feared to have been a heart attack proved to be extreme anxiety. She stayed with him in the emergency room.

Having been informed at the station of the incident, Detective Darrell Knight showed up a little while later. After speaking to Ramona and Charlie, the detective asked to see Fesche, but was informed he was in surgery. Instead, he asked to see the gunman's personal effects.

In the pocket of Fesche's jacket was a cell phone. Knight return-called the last number.

A man's voice answered. 'Tell me it's done,' he said.

'Hmm?' Knight mumbled.

'Dammit, Fesche, tell me it's done. Tell me Ramona Rios is dead.'

'Am I speaking with . . . ?'

'This is Cantone! Who else would it be

on this line? What is wrong with — '

Immediately, Nick Cantone stopped talking.

After several seconds, he said, 'Fesche?'

Knight cut off the call. A few seconds later the phone rang again, but the detective did not answer. Pulling a plastic evidence bag from his pocket, he dropped the phone into it.

★   ★   ★

When the police arrived at Adam Henry's Bel Air home at eight the next morning, he invited them in for breakfast and asked if they had a photographer with them. Once it was explained to him why they were there, he denied everything, including a couple of charges that were never mentioned. As he was being transported to the police station in handcuffs, Henry was heard to mutter, 'Damn you, Mac,' over and over again, and then he began to cry.

At the same time, officers arrived at both the home and the office of Nick Cantone, finding him at neither. He was finally tracked to the Santa Monica airport and was taken into custody minutes before boarding a private airplane with his attorney. They were planning to escape to South America. Even after having been read his rights, and having been warned by his lawyer to shut up, Cantone refused to remain silent, telling the arresting officers, 'You'll all be sorry. You have no *idea* what I can do.'

By noon, his attorney had quit.

* * *

Having been kept overnight for observation, Charlie Grosvenor was released from the hospital at nine in the morning. Detective Darrell Knight was waiting for him.

'How are you feeling, Governor?' he asked.

'All things considered, not too bad. Where's the girl?'

'My guess is she's calling every TV station in town to start a bidding war over exclusive rights to the biggest story to hit L.A. in years.'

Knight's cell phone rang.

'Yeah,' he said into it. 'Okay, good.' Hanging up, he told Charlie, 'We've got them both. Henry and Cantone.'

'Cantone?'

'The billionaire developer who owns half of downtown and wants the other half. He was the one who hired Fesche to kill Ramona. Seems he didn't like that she was starting to ask questions about his plans to run the city. He's still acting like he has executive privilege but it seems his friend Henry is launching a new career as a singer. Which leads me to my next point. I'm going to need you to come down to the station to make an official report.'

'I can do that,' Charlie said.

Knight yawned.

'Sorry,' he said. 'I've been at it all night. Still wearing the same clothes from yesterday.'

'You'll be one of us soon.'

'Yeah,' Knight said, grinning. 'When my wife throws me out for never being home, I'll be sure to look you up on Skid Row. I'll tell you one thing, Governor. I wish I had been able to figure this thing out like you did. I'll get the hosannas from the department since I can close the cases on what looked like six random murders: those four homeless men, the cabbie, and a hired killer, plus a thirty-year-old cold case. But it's all because of what you and Ramona Rios discovered.'

'Oh, well, maybe we got lucky.'

'Yeah. Or maybe you're both part bloodhound. Look, I don't suppose there's any way you'd consider — '

'Damn!' Charlie suddenly shouted. 'All this excitement, I forgot about Pooch!'

'Who's Pooch?'

'I have a dog now. He adopted me. He's been home alone all night. I have to go put some food down. Damn, do I have any food for him? I've gotta go take care of my dog. I'll come by the station later.'

'Tell you what, Governor. I'll drive you home. And I still find it puzzling that you have a home, but you don't need to tell me about it if you don't want to. Then we'll go to the station.'

On the way to Charlie's apartment, he said, 'I'm rich, that's what it's about.'

'Sorry?' Knight said.

'I'm rich, Detective. I'm worth millions. I won the Lotto several years back. Nobody knows that, 'cept you, now, and Ramona. At least she knows part of it.'

'Why in God's name do you stay on the streets, then?'

'To help people. That, and . . . hell, this is going to sound crazy to you, but Skid Row's my home now. I've been there so long, I don't know where else to go. With all the news coverage that's going to result from this mess, I really hope my cover isn't blown.'

'I'll do what I can to keep you out of it. You should probably talk to Ramona about that, too.'

When Charlie got home, Pooch started running in circles, becoming so excited he peed a little on the floor. 'That's alright, boy, you've earned the right to be excited,' Charlie said. After taking the dog out back to do his business, Charlie set down some fresh water and opened a can of beef stew for the dog.

'Damn spoiled dog's never gonna accept plain dog food after this,' Charlie told Detective Knight, with a smile.

Epilogue

Mayor Alberto Soto looked to be a shoo-in for re-election in November. His campaign was based on the idea of establishing residential hotels for the homeless in Skid Row, particularly since the Phoenix Terrace development had been cancelled and the space was available.

Nick Cantone and Adam Henry remained in jail pending trial on conspiracy to murder. In addition, the family of Deborah Questal, the young victim of the hit-and-run murder thirty years earlier, had engaged an attorney and filed a wrongful death civil suit against Henry. The story was rarely out of the news.

Gunnar Fesche had opted to turn the state's evidence against Cantone in return for a reduced sentence for the murder of Alex Tunzi. He was spending his time not in jail, but in secured rehab, learning how to walk again.

After much deliberation, Ramona Rios

agreed to return to KPAC as its morning co-anchor. While her working relationship with the station's news director, Robert Bauman, remained professional, but cool, she was developing a friendship with the station's new manager, Martha Agajanian. The latter had replaced station manager Jason Hulme, who was relocated by ComCorp to a station in Boise. All the other anchors and reporters at Channel 8 had started referring to her on-air as 'our own Ramona Rios.'

While it was not a planned thing, she told a writer who was profiling her for *Los Angeles Magazine* that she was thinking of legally changing her first name to *Arone*.

The governor was seen less and less on the street. Most of the other streeters figured it was because of his age — if they worried about it at all. The governor was still available to pass a spare quarter or Washington on to anyone who needed it, but he was also spending more time at home with Pooch.

He had even bought himself a television.

What nobody knew was that Charlie

was also working as an unpaid advisor to Mayor Soto's office on the project to reform the row.

Nobody except Ramona Rios, who kept it to herself.

About once a month, Ramona snuck her way over to his apartment, dressing down as best she could to blend in, just to see how he was doing. Sometimes, she arrived with a shopping bag of dog food.

'You know something, baby girl,' he said during one such visit, 'I'm not going to last forever.'

'Don't talk about that,' Ramona said.

'Let me say my piece. Nobody knows what's going to happen to them, and I'm no spring chicken. I have a meeting with my attorney tomorrow to put my affairs in order and make out a will.'

'Charlie . . . '

'Don't worry, I'm not dying, or anything like that. I'm just getting older, and now that you know my secret, you know all that money has to go somewhere. I'm planning on establishing a foundation to help streeters, but that's neither here nor there. What I'm asking you is whether, when the time comes, you'd take the most valuable thing I've got.'

'What's that?'

Charlie nodded toward Pooch, who was resting on the floor in front of them. The dog's tail began to thump.

'Of course I will,' Ramona said. 'But not for a long, long time.'

'It's a deal, then. If you've got the time, what do you say to dinner at TiJacques?'

A week later, the governor was on the job, sitting on a battered folding chair on San Pedro Street, watching the world shuffle by. An unmarked police car pulled up and Detective Darrell Knight got out.

'Detective,' the governor said.

'Governor. Can I talk to you a second?'

'Sure. What's up?'

'Adam Henry's trial has been scheduled. They're expediting it because his mental health is failing. Everybody thought he was just a dimwit, but it turns out he's been suffering from the early stages of Alzheimer's disease.'

'Damn.'

'Anyway, you'll be required to testify. I just wanted you to know that.'

'I understand.'

'Here's the thing. There's probably no way to protect your secret on the stand. Your financial situation is going to come out, most likely through cross examination. I'm sorry.'

'Yeah, well . . . maybe it's time to retire anyway.'

'Just wanted to warn you.'

'Appreciate it.'

Knight looked around and scratched the back of his neck.

'Okay,' the governor said, 'what else is on your mind?'

'Well, we've had a report of a disappearance. A young girl from a rich, influential family . . . very rich, very influential . . . who got into the drug scene and then vanished. Since the department now thinks I can work miracles, thanks to you, I'm getting leaned on to solve the case.' Knight pulled a photograph of a blonde, freckled, pouty-faced young woman. 'This is her, Audrey Chandler. If you happen to see her down here, or even hear anything

271

about a new girl on the block, I'd appreciate a call.'

The governor studied the photo.

'I'll let you know, Detective,' he said.